Strike At The Giant

Strike At The Giant

Jim Harrington

Dover and Blackstone Media L.L.C.
Pittsburgh, PA USA

Strike At The Giant

Dover and Blackstone Media L.L.C.

For information address:
Dover and Blackstone Media L.L.C.
P.O. Box 12944
Pittsburgh, PA 15244-0944
www.doverandblackstone.com

ISBN: 978-0-9841160-1-0
Printed in the United States of America

Chapter One

Hasan Azzam stared at the large, shiny clean airplane that was parked on the tarmac, at gate 36, of the Pittsburgh International Airport. A luggage valet rolled by his food service truck and he slouched a bit in his seat, pulling down the brim of his baseball cap. No one was paying any attention to him. They all had their own jobs to do. The planes had to be loaded and sent on their way. He could have looked like Osama bin Laden himself and no one would have paid him any mind. He grinned a little. Could it be this easy? Where was all this Homeland Security everyone had talked about? He and his cohorts had entered the United States with absolutely no problem. Of course they arrived at different places and at staggered times, but there were no obstructions. They had laughed when they recalled the story of one conspirator who had inadvertently carried a small Swiss Army knife, on a key chain, through customs and had not been stopped.

Hasan looked around to see if his three friends were in place. This would be simple. There would be no hijackers this time. This would be a statement, pure and simple. One man would transport the package into the plane's storage compartment, while Hasan and the two other men kept a lookout for airport security. The explosive would be armed and set to trigger long after the men had left the scene…. possibly, depending upon departure time, while the jetliner was in the air. Americans would see that they could be attacked anywhere and at any time. Soon 9-11 would become just another day in a long list of nightmarish days. Hasan was sure the revolution would be victorious. How could it not be? Allah and his legions of faithful were on their side. Soon the infidels would be brought to their knees. It was what he'd been taught so many years before and it was what he believed.

Four men, one small cell, were about to strike fear into the hearts of all Americans. Hasan watched as his friend with the package drove another utility vehicle up next to the loading conveyor. He looked so calm, so normal. They all had the proper uniforms and credentials. They had studied maps of the airport and they knew what was behind every door and security gate. They had become explosives experts and were confident in the reliability and effectiveness of their weapon. It would obliterate the Boeing 767 and everything that was on it. But first things first. The bomb would be placed and primed and the passengers would be boarded. The team would leave the airport, individually, and meet again at a small motel a mile or so away. They would change, switch cars and drive as a group to Cleveland. All the while, they would monitor the news, listening for reports on their devastating attack. In Cleveland, they would take different modes of transportation to Toronto where they would meet at a safe house and wait until things quieted down. It was so simple, so fool proof. Hasan had wanted so desperately to be the one who placed the bomb. He wanted to be the lead man, the one to carry the sword. But this time around it was not to be. As a matter of fact, he had drawn the safest position, the one furthest from the plane. This was not a challenge for a man of Hasan's courage, but he knew that the success of the mission depended upon the cooperation of all the participants. He would have his day, just not this day.

The point man stepped on to the tarmac and casually eyed his friends. He walked to the back of the vehicle and pulled two suitcases from a rack. He turned and started his walk to the loading belt. With all of their preparation and planning, who would have thought that the man would step directly in front of a passing fuel truck? Suddenly, there was a massive explosion. Everything near the detonation was engulfed in a large ball of flames, including the plane, the man with the bomb, and Hasan's two other lookout friends. Hasan, however, was far enough away to miss the brunt of the explosion, although his truck was scorched and the windshield shattered.

He sat motionless, unable to comprehend what had just happened. One moment he was a team member, part of a righteous assault group, and the next he was alone. Then the sounds of the real world began to fade in: screams, engines and sirens. He took a cleansing breath, started his truck, shifted into gear and carefully started to drive away. Everywhere he looked he could see flashing lights and emergency vehicles. Police and fire personnel were all around him. He kept going, slowly, deliberately so as not to attract any attention.

The small abandoned access road at the far end of runway 28 was his escape route. It was remote and surprisingly unsecured. He pulled the truck into a grove of trees, stopped and shut off the engine. Now what? They had only discussed the possibility of failure once and it was summarily dismissed. Their plan was so simple and so foolproof. Yet it had failed and the rest of his team was dead. He took a rag from under the front seat and wiped everything on the truck that he thought he and his allies had handled. They had stolen the truck, so there was no other way that it could be traced back to Hasan. He walked another hundred yards to the place where they had hidden their Honda CRV. He found the keys where he had left them, under a nearby rock, opened the driver's side door and got in.

He thought for a second; the backup plan in the event of failure. He got out of the SUV, walked to the back and opened the tailgate door. He lifted the carpeting and pulled up on the 'picnic table' door. Underneath were a small safe and an assortment of weapons, including a high powered, collapsible, sniper rifle complete with carrying case. He examined several keys on his key chain until he found the right one and then pulled the safe box out on to the floor of the car. He scanned the area nervously to see if anyone was approaching. All he could hear was the noise from the activity at the site of the explosion and that was a long way off. He keyed the box and it popped open. He didn't know what he'd find. No one ever dreamed that they'd need to use it.

It was getting dark and he needed to use a small flashlight to clearly see the contents of the container. What was this? Two large envelopes! He ripped one open and found five thousand dollars. It would be a start, but hardly enough to sustain and rebuild the cell. The other envelope was thinner and contained a few typewritten sheets of paper.

He read them carefully. It was a list of do's and don'ts. Do not go back to the motel. Abandon anything and everything you left in your room. The planned escape to Toronto was off. He was to drive to the Holiday Inn in Pittsburgh's South Hills and go directly to room 420. It was already booked and the key was taped to the sheet of paper. He would find additional instructions in a briefcase in that room. It was a bit cryptic, but a place to start. He put everything back, except a loaded 9mm Berretta and five hundred dollars. He placed the gun under the front seat and the money into his coat pocket. Then he started the car and headed for the hotel.

Pittsburgh isn't a big city, but the region's road system is a mess. The topography is that of steep hills and menacing ridges. One can never anticipate the length of a trip by 'the way the crow flies'. In most cities, ten miles would take fifteen to twenty minutes, on a good highway, at fifty-five miles an hour. In Pittsburgh, ten miles might take forty-five minutes to an hour, depending upon traffic and the road conditions. Hasan was new to the area. He had only slipped across the Canadian-US border a few weeks earlier. Now, he found himself questioning why he had made the trip in the first place. When he walked the abandoned logging road that snaked its way into the country, he was full of energy and confidence. Now, as he drove away from the airport, he felt doubt, uncertainty and, for the first time since he started his jihad, fear.

It took him nearly two hours to find the Holiday Inn. Hasan pulled into a space directly in front of the older hotel. He turned off the motor and looked at the building. It was so, so American looking. Why had they picked this place, he wondered? It wasn't convenient to anything, certainly not to the airport. One would have to drive secondary highways to get to a major interstate. If you asked him, this was not a good choice for the rendezvous, but then, no one asked him.

He reached over the front seat and retrieved an overnight bag. He opened it and stuffed the envelopes and 9mm inside. He looked into the rearview mirror, straightened his hair, made sure he looked presentable, got out of the car and walked into the hotel. There was already a room waiting for him so there was no need to stop at the front desk. He had mastered the art of delivering his English without so much as a trace of a Middle Eastern accent, but he still felt awkward pretending to be an American. It felt so hypocritical smiling and laughing with these Americans, when in reality, all he wanted to do, his sole purpose for living, was to kill as many of them as possible. He walked to the elevator and pushed the 'up' button. A few other guests gathered quietly around him. There he was, smiling and trying to look pleasant. If they only knew, he thought. He was the very thing these people feared the most, a real live terrorist. He was right there, in their midst and they didn't have a clue.

The elevator door opened and he stepped aside, politely allowing the others to enter first. "Thank you!" one person said. "You're welcome," Hasan replied. It was not an express trip. There was a passenger or two for each of the three floors prior to the fourth. But he was the only person to exit on to that floor. The sign in front of the elevator indicated that 420 was to the right, just a few doors down. He sensed an uneasy silence. He had stayed in enough hotels to recognize the hallway sounds, multiple TVs, indistinguishable conversation and the rumble of the ice machine.

When he reached 420, he paused and put his ear to the door. Again there wasn't a sound. He inserted his room key and unlocked the door. He placed his hand inside his overnight bag and took hold of the Berretta. He pushed the door open but didn't enter the room. He listened again. Suddenly a door opened down the hall and he turned quickly in that direction. A man and a woman stepped into the hallway, dressed as if they were on their way to dinner. They had no idea how close they had come to being shot. The couple walked by Hasan, hardly noticing his presence. He watched them as they passed and he thought how arrogant, affluent and self-absorbed they looked. He almost shot them for the heck of it.

As quickly as they had entered his world, they were gone and the hallway was empty again. He looked back to the room, held the handgun a bit tighter and stepped inside. He closed the door, took out the 9mm and dropped the bag to the floor. At first glance, the layout appeared fairly standard. To his right was a bathroom. He looked in and saw that the shower curtain was drawn on the bathtub. He entered and pulled it open, anticipating the worst. It was newly cleaned and empty. Other than the bathroom there weren't very many places for someone to hide. The closet was a recess in the wall with an open clothes rod and no door. The two beds were on floor pedestals so nothing could be placed under them. And there was no one hiding behind the furniture. There was no one else in the room. He was alone. He retrieved the carrying bag and emptied its contents on one of the beds. He didn't have much. Besides the envelopes and the Glock, it contained a change of underwear, another shirt, a pair of Dockers, some socks and a thin jacket.

He walked to the easy chair and sat down. Now what, he wondered. The instructions didn't say what the next step would be. This didn't surprise the young man. When he trained in Afghanistan, he was told that information was valuable and must be protected. Never tell the group the entire plan and never put to paper the part of the plan that you're given. You were trained to memorize everything. If it was in writing, you were instructed to read it, learn it and destroy the hard copy. He looked at the information in the envelope again, made sure that he hadn't missed anything and then tore it into small pieces. He'd flush it down the toilet when he got up. Now he would lean back and close his eyes. He was surprisingly tired and it had been a disastrous day. He thought about his friends who had died. He had trained for death but was amazed at how fast it could take you. One second they were there and the next they were with Allah. How lucky they were, Hasan thought.

Then he thought of the mission and how they had failed. Everything had been going so well. They were only minutes away from success and suddenly it was over! He knew that he had to redeem himself and turn the defeat into a victory before he would be able to face his comrades again. But how? He was alone, with limited funds in a strange city. He needed help. Training had also taught him that no member of the group would be abandoned. He looked out the room's window. "Ah, but where are you?" he thought. Did they even know he was there? He placed the gun on the nightstand next to the chair, turned his head and fell deeply asleep.

Chapter Two

Jack Kane had come to Pittsburgh from New York to attend an awards dinner for his friend Detective Thomas Caputo, who had been awarded the Distinguished Service Medal by the Pennsylvania state police. Through a strange set of circumstances, Kane and Caputo had joined forces to put an end to the sophisticated and lucrative Argari organized crime ring. In the process, the men had killed one of the country's deadliest assassins, Johnny Reece. The hit man was, of all things, a major league baseball pitcher and, as if that weren't enough, an All-Star. He was devious, diabolical and now deceased. In the end, this twenty game winner was a loser.

Like all of the awards dinners he had ever attended, this one was long-winded and predictable. He should have had all the time in the world for Tom to drive him to the airport for his return flight home. But the ceremony had rambled on and by the time it finished, they were running way behind. Even with lights and sirens, they'd be cutting it close.

The baggage check-in was slow and security was understaffed. Kane looked at his watch and then to his friend, Caputo, who was waiting with him until he cleared security and was on his way.

"I'm never going to make it, Tom. It leaves in five minutes."

"I'm sorry, Jack. I don't know what to say. I thought you'd have all the time in the world!"

"I...."

Suddenly there was a loud noise and everything in the building shuddered. Instinctively everyone crouched down.

"What was that?" Caputo yelled over the commotion.

"Something blew up, if you ask me."

"Something very big just blew up," Caputo continued.

Everyone waited for a moment to see if there would be more explosions. Then the entire group slowly got to their feet. The screeners and security guards began to cordon off the entrance. There wouldn't be anyone entering or exiting the terminal now until they had determined where that explosion had come from.

Caputo and Kane walked over to a security guard, who was already surrounded by a large crowd of anxious travelers.

"I have a plane to catch and it leaves in ten minutes!" one young lady said in a loud and excited voice.

"Me too!" another chimed in.

"I'm sorry folks, we're in a lockdown." the guard yelled. "The good news is you won't miss your planes because nothing's coming in or flying out of this airport until we know what's going on."

Caputo pulled his badge and showed it to the man. The three men walked a few steps away from the group.

"I'm a detective with the state police. What's going on?"

"Well detective, I don't know much more than you! I just got a radio report saying that the plane at gate 36 blew up!"

"It what?" Caputo asked again, as if he couldn't comprehend it the first time.

"Blew up," he repeated, "at the gate."

"Did you say gate 36?" Kane asked while looking at his boarding pass.

"That's right," said the guard.

"There goes my luggage," Kane said.

"That was your flight?" Caputo asked.

Kane showed him the ticket. "Yup, that was it." He pointed to the number, "Gate 36. It was the flight to New York."

"Well I don't think anybody will be flying to New York tonight, not from this airport," said the security guard.

"We need to get back there," Caputo said, pointing beyond the security checkpoint.

"I don't know," the guard was unsure. "And who's your friend?"

"Detective Jack Kane, NYPD retired. Show him some ID Jack."

Kane pulled out his wallet and flashed an ID and his honorary shield.

"Yeah, but he's retired. I don't know."

"Well I'm not retired and he's with me," Caputo said as he took Kane by the arm and started for the airside terminal. "Now we've got work to do."

Surprisingly, the guard simply said, "Okay." and let them continue.

Caputo walked past the people mover that shuttled people from the landside to the airside terminal.

"They won't be using that for a while. We'll have to walk." Caputo said.

"You know something always happens to me when I visit this city." Kane said trying to keep up with the younger man. "There's never a dull moment."

The two men walked to a maintenance exit that led to the outside.

"This should take us where we want to go."

"Should we really be getting involved?" Kane questioned. "You know that guard back there shouldn't have let us through."

"Yeah, I know. I think we caught him off balance."

"Well, he may lose his job."

"Nah, no one will know."

"What do you mean? There are security cameras all over this place. When they review them, he'll be toast."

"Well then, think of it as a security check and that guy failed. I mean, do you really want a guy like that guarding your airport? We just did the community a service."

"Great, the guy's gonna lose his job." Kane shook his head. "That makes me feel terrible."

"He's not going to lose his job. I'm a state police officer and I have a right to be here. And you, you're my deputy."

"Deputy!"

"All right, my consultant. Is that better?" Caputo pushed open the door and stepped outside.

"Consultant! You gotta be kidding. You know the old expression, 'those who can, do, those who can't, teach, and those who can't teach, consult." Kane said, shaking his head.

"Okay, so you're my dad."

"You know, consultant does have a ring to it."

They were both outside now. The Landside Terminal and the Airside Terminal at Pittsburgh International Airport are connected by a sub-runway computerized rail system. Normally, the ride from one terminal to the other took about two minutes. Walking from one to the other was a ten-minute adventure. The problem wasn't just the distance; it was maneuvering around and dodging all the obstacles that separated the two facilities. There were luggage trains and maintenance caddies, fuel tankers and catering trucks, and they all seemed to be coming from different directions.

"Are they aiming at us?" Kane asked.

"It does seem like we have targets on our backs, doesn't it?" Caputo agreed. "No, that explosion's got everyone acting a little nuts, I'm afraid."

"It's amazing these guys don't kill someone."

"Yeah, well the night is still young."

"And I thought the streets of New York were dangerous."

"They are Jack, they are."

They could see the glow from the fire on the opposite side of the building, as they approached the Airside Terminal. The noise from the commotion became louder, too.

"Should we walk around?" Kane asked.

Caputo pointed to a door. "No, it'll be quicker if we go straight through."

Moments later the two men were heading down concourse B toward Gate 36. It seemed that everyone in the airport was walking in the opposite direction and that they were the only people headed toward the fire.

"There aren't going to be too many travelers leaving from this airport tonight," said Kane. "It looks like they're all going home."

"Yeah, well I guess the sight of a burning jet airliner can make you change your travel plans. Suddenly flying doesn't seem all that appealing."

The walk from one end of the concourse to the other took about ten more minutes. The only things fast at an airport are the planes, everything else takes time. At last they were there, Caputo showed his credentials to a few people and explained Kane's presence and then the men started to snoop around, Caputo going in one direction and Kane moving in another. First, Kane looked through the large plate glass windows, to the burning airplane not too far away. Then he looked up at the unbroken glass pane.

"Amazing that it's not in a million pieces, don't you think?" asked a relatively attractive and smartly dressed young woman who was standing just to his right.

"You would think the blast would have blown these things away," Kane agreed, as he tapped his knuckles against the glass.

"They're designed to do just what they did. They're shatterproof."

"No kidding!" Kane was impressed.

"They probably could have taken a blast three times this size."

The woman extended her hand.

"Sandy Ryan, FBI. And who might you be?"

"I'm Jack Kane, NYPD, retired."

"Retired!"

"Yeah, well actually I'm here as a consultant."

"Consultant?"

"Yeah, to the state police," he pointed to Caputo. "I'm working the case with Tom Caputo. He's right over there."

"Oh, I see." She stepped a little closer, "So what's your initial impression?"

Kane started to walk along the window to get a better angle of the plane. Sandy followed him step for step.

"Initial impression! I don't know."

"They said that they think static electricity set off the fuel truck and it, in turn, blew up the plane. It went off right under the left wing, and those wings are nothing more than large fuel tanks."

"I've never heard of that happening before, have you?" Kane asked.

"That truck didn't blow up by itself."

Simultaneously, Kane and Ryan turned to a little old lady who was seated in a wheelchair right behind them.

"I didn't mean to be eavesdropping, but I couldn't help but overhear your conversation."

"You saw what happened?" Kane said.

"Yep. I was looking out the window, right there where you're standing."

"Has anyone talked with you?" asked Ryan.

"Other than you, no."

"What did you see?" Kane continued.

"Well, it happened really fast but, that fuel truck had just driven around the front of the plane and was heading toward the wing when this fella got off one of those luggage train things." She paused, remembering something else, "Hmmm, the strange thing was that, with all the bags he was pulling on that cart, he was only carrying one."

"Carrying one what?" Ryan pressed.

"One package the size of a large shoe box," she paused again, and looked at Ryan and Kane who were wide-eyed, waiting for the rest of her story, "when he stepped in front of the fuel truck."

"Intentionally?" Ryan asked.

"I don't think so. It sure didn't look intentional. I mean, it might have been, but it looked like he was preoccupied. I saw him glance in three separate directions just before he took his last step."

Kane looked to Ryan and then back to the lady.

"You're sure about this."

"Absolutely. You see, I really can't move around too much in this thing," she said referring to the wheelchair, "so I've become a professional observer. I see everything, and nobody really pays any attention to me. I think the wheelchair makes people uncomfortable. The truck wasn't the first thing to explode. It was the box he was carrying, when it hit the ground. A moment later the fuel truck burst into flames and then the airplane went up. It was amazing, like something in the movies. Everyone was running all over the place, ducking, screaming, and I was glued to the action like it was on HBO."

"You said he looked in three directions," Ryan stated. "Did you see what he was looking at?"

"Well, I can't be sure. It's purely a guess on my part, but it looked like he was looking at three men."

"Three men! Where?" Kane asked.

"One on the other side of the wing, the other near the front of the plane and I think the other one was in a truck."

"What kind of truck?" Kane asked wanting more.

"It looked like one of those box trucks that rise up in the air."

"You mean a catering truck?"

"Yes, that's it, a catering truck."

Sandy looked out at the wreckage. "I don't see any burning catering trucks out there."

"Oh, he took off," she added. "He left right after the explosion. The other two men weren't so lucky, I'm afraid. They didn't know what hit them. I'm sure you'll find their bodies, or what's left of them, right down there." She was pointing toward the burning airplane.

"Thank you for this information, Miss…???"

"Thompson, and that's Mrs., Mrs. Judy Thompson."

Sandy motioned to another detective and he hurried over.

"Charlie, will you do me a favor and take all of Mrs. Thompson's contact information. She's been a big help and we're going to want to talk with her again."

"Sure Sandy." he replied. Ryan took Kane by the arm and the two began to walk.

"Now, what are your first impressions?"

"An act of terrorism. The guy had high explosives in the box. But then again what do I know?"

"Don't kid yourself, Mr. Kane. I know exactly who you are."

"You do?" asked Kane.

"Yes I do. I've read all about your exploits in the paper."

"You shouldn't believe everything you read in the paper."

The young woman smiled.

"Well, frankly I don't believe everything I read in the newspapers, but I was also at the banquet for Tom Caputo this evening. I heard your talk and the nice words people said about you."

Kane was following Sandy's lead and she was walking down the ramp at gate 35.

"I must be slipping. In the old days I would have seen an attractive woman like you in the crowd."

"Thank you, Jack. I don't feel slighted. You were very busy."

"Any time I have to get up in front of a crowd, I'm in another world until it's over. You mind telling me where we're going?"

Sandy took hold of the door handle at the end of the ramp and pushed it open.

"We're going to check out the scene of the crime and see if we can find any catering trucks"

The younger woman scurried down the steep set of stairs while Kane followed behind, slowed by his middle aged body and the effects of a recent meniscus knee surgery.

"Ah, to be twenty years younger," he said to Ryan at the bottom of the stairs. "I was in great shape back in those days."

"Ah, to be twenty years older," she grinned, "I'd be so much wiser right now."

"Point well taken. I guess we're never satisfied where we are in life, are we?" asked Kane.

The couple walked over to gate 36 and the first thing Kane noticed wasn't the carnage. It was the smell. It was an acrid, sour mix of jet fuel, melted plastic and burnt electrical wiring. Then, of course, there was the smell of scorched human bodies, one so horribly distinctive, it easily cut through to the forefront of the odors. It reminded him of Vietnam and burning helicopters, of charred bodies and scenes that could only be found in the midst of the horrors of war. Those memories, he thought, were long forgotten. He was surprised at how wrong he was.

"No sign of any catering truck."

"No, if the motor was still running, and he was involved, he's long gone now."

Sandy continued to pan the scene. "Do you have any idea how many catering trucks work this airport? It'll take us forever to find this guy."

"It shouldn't be that bad. How many catering trucks will be rolling around this airport with scorch marks on the front end? Heck, when this baby went, it probably blistered the truck's paint job."

"What makes you say that?"

Kane pointed to the terminal siding. "Take a look at the paint on the side of the building. Some of it got burned away and it's at least twenty-five feet beyond where that truck would have been."

Kane went on, "And I'd be looking for a vehicle with a smashed windshield. The glass on the terminal may have been designed to take a powerful blast, but regular old car safety glass would have cracked like an egg."

Ryan paused, "You know, you're right!"

"I know I'm right." Kane said as he brushed some soot from his coat sleeve.

Kane started for the epicenter of the explosion and Ryan followed.

"What do you think, Al Qaeda?"

"Probably, or one of their brother organizations. They're sneaky bastards and I wouldn't put it past them to do something cowardly, like this."

"I thought they worked in bigger groups."

"Yeah, well ever since we started dropping bunker buster bombs on their little hideouts in Afghanistan, I heard enlistment has dropped way off." Kane eyed something and kneeled on one knee, to get a better look. "I also read recently that our intelligence thought that they had gone to smaller cells. They're faster, easier to operate and expendable."

"Expendable?"

"Yup, that's the word they used."

"Isn't it nice to feel like you're a part of a team," Sandy said facetiously.

"You have to remember, Detective Ryan, these are the same wonderful people who brought you the suicide bomber, a truly unique and effective weapon of terror."

Kane was still focused on the pile of rubble in front of him. Ryan went on. "You think this might have been a suicide bombing?"

"Maybe," he replied, "but I don't think so." He took a pen from his coat pocket, reached down and retrieved what looked like the face of a small digital watch. "How many suicide bombers have timers on their bombs? Usually they just get in place and pull the chord."

"What do you think, it was an accident?" Ryan asked.

"Well, it was an accident when it went off. They probably planned on putting it in the plane's cargo compartment and driving away."

Ryan was pulling on some plastic gloves. "And what? The guy stepped in front of the truck?"

Kane stood up. "Hey these guys were hyped up. They weren't thinking straight. They were on an adrenaline high. The one with the bomb probably looked for his friends, saw that they were in place and hopped off that luggage tractor." He gestured toward the charred remains of the small vehicle and its two trailers of smoldering luggage. "You know, I was supposed to take this flight."

Sandy turned to Kane. "I didn't know that!"

"My luggage is probably right in there," he said, pointing to the burned bags.

They were quiet for a moment and then Sandy continued, "Do you think any of the others got away?"

"It's hard to say, but based upon Mrs. Thompson's statement, three out of the four disintegrated upon detonation. The fourth, our catering friend, was the only lucky one. He was far enough away and shielded by the truck. That monster still walks among us."

"There you are!" a voice interrupted. It was Caputo. "I thought I'd lost you."

Kane turned to his friend. "Sandy Ryan of the Federal

Bureau of Investigation, I'd like you to meet...."

"Hi Tom," she finished.

"Hey Sandy, how did you enjoy the banquet?"

"The chicken was delicious."

"I should have known," Kane said. "Who don't you know, Tom?"

"Sandy and I go way back, Jack. As a matter of fact there was a time when she had a crush on me."

Sandy poked Caputo in the arm. "It was you who had the crush on me, Tom Caputo."

"Maybe you're right. Thank God we didn't share the same recess."

"Recess!" said Kane.

"We went to school together, starting in third grade," Sandy finished.

"She had great pigtails in those days, Jack."

"And he had a nice chubby face."

Caputo looked up at the smoldering plane.

"It didn't take them long to put it out."

"The fire company is just across the runway and they practice dousing these things every day," she said. "They probably were here and had it out within ten minutes. They just bury the thing in foam. That's the soap suds you're standing in."

Jake turned to Caputo. "Did you find anything?"

"No, not really. Most people ducked, ran or crapped in their pants when this thing blew. Boy, it stinks out here doesn't it?"

"Yeah, and it'll be with you for a while. Why don't we commandeer one of these utility vehicles and take a cruise around the airport and see if we can find a catering truck with a singed paint job and a broken windshield?"

"Don't have to 'commandeer' anything. My car's just around the corner." Sandy said. "You know, if it were me, I'd head for the outskirts of the airport. I wouldn't risk trying to leave through a terminal."

"I agree," Kane said.

"You mind telling me why we're looking for a catering truck with a bad paint job?"

"I'll tell you when we're rolling."

And in a few minutes, they were in Sandy's car and Kane was doing just that. Pittsburgh International Airport is a big and busy facility. Thousands of travelers pass through its gates on a daily basis. It was nighttime and the runways were surrounded by a wooded perimeter. They would need some luck to find that truck.

"We've been doing this for over an hour, guys. What do you think? We gonna find this thing or what?" Sandy asked.

"If it's damaged, there's a good chance he ditched it. Let's give it a little while longer."

Just then, they got lucky. Their headlights flashed on what looked like the remnants of an abandoned service road.

"Well, we missed that the first time around." Kane pointed to the path. Sandy slowed the car and turned on to the old road.

"This hasn't been used for some time," she said.

Then their car lights reflected off of the hidden vehicle's taillights. "Bingo!" Kane slapped his hands together. "I think we've found our caterer."

Sandy stopped the car directly behind the truck. Caputo and Ryan got out and pulled their service revolvers. The unarmed 'consultant' Kane stepped from the car holding a flashlight.

"I think he's long gone. Unless he was hurt, he kept moving," Kane said as he panned the area with the beam of the flashlight.

"Yeah, there's no one here," Caputo said. Ryan and Caputo were now in the truck.

"But this is the truck. The windshield's cracked and there's burn marks all over the front of this thing," Sandy said as she examined the outside front end of the truck.

"Hey, get a load of this." Kane was examining something in the path.

"What have you got?" asked Caputo.

"It's a bit muddy over here."

"We just had two days of rain," Sandy interjected.

"Well I think we have his footprints," Kane said as he leaned over to get a closer look. He aimed the light toward the truck. "Yup, that's what we've got and they come from the truck."

"I think we'd better get a crew out here to go over this place before we mess something up and lose some evidence,"

Sandy said as she pulled her two-way from her coat pocket.

"Good idea." Caputo agreed.

Kane knelt down next to the footprints and moved the light back and forth along the impressions.

"The game is afoot," he mumbled.

"What did you say Jack?" asked Caputo

"One man and he's running. I think I'll be staying in Pittsburgh a little while longer." Kane answered in a clear and distinct voice.

Chapter Three

Hasan had been in a sound sleep. He would have slept longer, but something deep inside of him, that part that never rests, told him that he was not alone. As he was regaining consciousness, he slid his hand along the night table where he had placed his gun, but found nothing. Then he saw the man sitting on the bed, directly in front of him. When his eyes focused, he saw that the stranger was dressed in a Roman collar.

"A priest!" Hasan said in flawless English.

The man smiled. "Bless you my son." He was holding Hasan's weapon. "I didn't want you to wake up and shoot me."

"Who are you?" Hasan sat up in the chair. He was wide awake now.

"That's not important," the man replied. "Suffice it to say I'm the man who rented this room."

"You're our contact?"

The man placed the gun on the bed. "Our! What 'our'? You're alone. If I've got it right, Hasan, you blew it and your cohorts are with Allah."

"They're dead, but they died for the cause and even in death they were victorious."

"Oh stop it, will you." the stranger said. "Enough of the zealot crap. You botched it and that's why I'm here."

Wait, how did you know my name? I've never met you before."

The stranger took some pictures from his pocket and fanned them like a deck of cards in the direction of Hasan's face. "Four pictures, Hasan, but only one that matches you. I'm guessing that your friends died quickly."

Hasan lowered his head. "Very quickly."

The stranger paused for a moment and then continued.

"Well, if you've gotta go I guess that's the way to do it. There's nothing like a fast exit."

Hasan looked up at the man again. "Who are you and what's next? I take it you're not really one of us."

"Even your organization hires freelance professionals."

"Is that what you are, a freelance professional?"

"I'm the best there is, Hasan."

Suddenly Hasan felt a cold chill. He leaned forward in the chair.

"So is the mission still on? Do we have orders?"

The man didn't say anything until he stood up.

"Hasan, they call me The Ghost."

"I've heard of you. You're a killer."

"Look who's talking!" the man laughed. "Hasan, in this business, we're all killers. Some of us just do it for different reasons. You do it for the hereafter and I do it for the here and now. You kill for God and I kill for money. We both kill, Hasan."

"My work is God's work and yours is Satan's," Hasan answered defensively.

"Oh, aren't we being a bit judgmental," the Ghost replied. "Ah, but I see there's no convincing you. Did you bring the bag?"

Hasan pointed to the overnight bag on the floor.

"Good job, Hasan," the Ghost said as he retrieved it and placed it on the bed. "We would have been lost without this."

Hasan looked confused. "What do you mean? It's only my overnight bag."

The Ghost smiled. "The one your superiors gave you?"

"Yes, that's the one."

"Well, that's the one I'm looking for." The Ghost pulled out a pen knife and sliced open the bottom of the bag, revealing a false bottom. When he pulled it back, he revealed four small metal vials seated in a foam-protected base.

"Well, it's the right bag," the Ghost grinned.

"What is that?" Hasan was completely surprised.

The Ghost hesitated, as if deciding whether or not to tell Hasan, and then explained. "These, my good man, are neuro-toxins."

"Neuro-toxins!"

"Yes, and some of the strongest known to man. A drop or two in a glass of water would create a vapor that would kill everyone within thirty feet of the glass."

"What about the person who did that? Wouldn't he die, too?"

"Nah. You take the antidote agent first, about an hour or so before you set the ball in motion. That's this stuff here," the Ghost held up another tube. "It's really great, Hasan. We've got some incredible people on our payroll right now. You'd be amazed. It's not black market crap developed by the Russians back in the eighties. No, this is state of the art. It's brand new. They won't know what hit 'em."

"We really do have a research team? I thought that they were just rumors. I didn't know!"

"Why would you?" the Ghost pushed the false bottom back into place, once again concealing the poison. "You don't need to know."

"But I know now." Hasan sounded calm, sensing for the first time that he was safe, trusted and part of the new scheme.

"Yes you do. Seeing that you were responsible for bringing it here, I felt that it was only fair that you should know."

Hasan shifted in the chair. "What's the plan? What are we hitting?"

"One thing at a time, Hasan, one thing at a time." The Ghost got up and walked to the room's refreshment refrigerator. "First, a little toast to your brave comrades." He took out two small wine bottles and unscrewed the caps.

"But it's against our faith."

"Your faith, Hasan, not mine. Remember, I'm a hired gun. Now, we're not back home in the Middle East. We're in the decedent US of A and how's the old saying go? When in Rome, do as the Romans do." His back was to the young terrorist, hiding the small pill that he palmed into Hasan's drink. He turned to him with both bottles in his hands. "Besides, I know that you've imbibed. All of you guys do, when you're on the road. Here." He handed him the tainted beverage and raised his own drink in a toast. "To the brave revolutionaries who gave their all to our noble cause."

Hasan paused for a moment. "To our cause? Don't you mean my cause?"

"Whatever," and the Ghost took a drink from his bottle. Hasan was beginning to feel contempt for this man, but the dead men were his friends, so he raised the bottle to his lips and took a generous swallow. The Ghost sat on the edge of the bed again and stared. Hasan took another drink of the sweet tasting wine. For some reason, the bottle seemed heavier. A minute passed and suddenly, to Hasan's surprise, the bottle slipped from his grip and dropped to the floor. His first instinct was to reach down and pick it up, but when he tried, he found that he couldn't move. He went to speak, but there wasn't any sound. All he could do was sit there and breathe.

"Ah, that wine does have a kick to it, doesn't it?" the Ghost said as he got up again and picked the bottle up off the floor, walked over to the room's sink and poured the remaining contents from both bottles down the drain. Then he rinsed them, put the caps back on and dropped them into the case. He took three new bottles from his coat pocket and placed two back into the fridge and one on the table next to Hasan. There was panic in the young man's eyes, but he could not move. There was nothing that he could do.

"Relax, Hasan. I'm afraid that this stuff won't wear off for another hour or so." The Ghost was methodical, every move well planned. He stripped down to his underwear and placed the priest garb on the bed. "Don't get nervous. I'm not going to molest you. I'm not that way. I just want your clothes." He pulled off the man's shoes and socks, then unbuckled his belt, unzipped his pants and removed them, too. He took his shirt and Hasan was sitting paralyzed in his underwear.

He looked at Hasan, grabbed a tissue from a box on the night table and wiped his lips. "You're drooling. I'm afraid there's really not much I can do about that."

Hasan sat there and watched the Ghost get into his clothes.

"Did any of you notice that you were all about the same size? No, probably not. You were picked for that reason. That way I was guaranteed an outfit that would fit me. The mission, Hasan, actually turned out better than I, we had imagined. You see, I would have had to deal with four of you, had you succeeded. Not that I couldn't have handled it, but this makes it easier and cleaner."

The Ghost was now standing fully dressed in Hasan's outfit.

"Now, it's your turn." And as quickly as he had dressed himself, he put the priest's suit on Hasan. "You probably think that this is a bit of a sacrilege, but think of it as a sacrifice for the greater good." He straightened the small crucifix on the coat lapel. "I'll bet this is the first time you've worn one of these," the Ghost said devilishly. "Well don't worry. You won't have to do it again."

Hasan grunted a disapproving sound. It was the best he could do.

"You feel a bit helpless there, don't you old boy?" The Ghost seemed to be enjoying this. "Actually, you should feel that way. You see, you're getting screwed and you can't even lean back and enjoy it."

The Ghost then went to a plastic bag that he had brought with him and took from it a magazine, full of pictures of child pornography. "Isn't this stuff disgusting?" he asked. "The guys who put this stuff together should have their balls cut off, don't you think?" Hasan's eyes widened and he made another wild sound.

"Absolutely. My sentiments exactly," said the Ghost as he snapped on a pair of surgical rubber gloves. He took a silencer from the bag and screwed it on to the barrel of Hasan's gun. Then he placed the opened magazine on the bed and turned to a particularly graphic and vulgar picture. "Hmmm, that should work." He stepped back, just to the right side of Hasan, carefully placed the weapon in to the man's limp hand, aimed and fired a silenced round into the magazine. "You're angry," he fired another shot into the pornography. "Now, you're really angry." He took a close look at

Hasan's shooting hand. "That should do it. You must have some gunpowder residue on your hands." He stepped back and looked at his victim. Hasan couldn't move, but his eyes gave away the fact that he understood what was going on. "Ah yes, Hasan, or should I say Father Hasan? When they find you, they'll assume that you're just some tortured soul, another pedophile priest who couldn't stand living with himself any longer. By the time they run a tox screen on you, the paralytic will have dissipated. Oh, and in case you're wondering, you don't have to be alive for it to do that."

The Ghost walked back to Hasan. "Open wide," he said as he pulled open the man's mouth and stuck the silencer in against Hasan's upper palate. "Give my regards to Allah. Hope you enjoy all those vestal virgins." He fired and the bullet tore apart the back of Hasan's head. The Ghost ducked away from some splatter. The dead man's body sagged and the life in his eyes disappeared. The slug had punctured a hole in the room's plate glass window and sailed off into the night.

"Isn't that convenient," said the Ghost. He placed the gun in Hasan's dead hand and let it drop into his lap. He took the bottle of wine from the night stand, opened it, downed a couple of drinks, wrapped Hasan's other hand around it so that there would be a good set of prints and then placed it on to the same spot where Hasan had dropped his bottle earlier. He removed the surgical gloves and tossed them into the overnight bag, He looked around the room to make sure that everything was the way that he wanted it to be. Yes. All appeared to be in order.

"Well, it's been real, Hasan ol' pal, but enough of this fun, I've got to run. Thanks for everything." The Ghost grabbed the bag, hurried to the door and was gone.

Chapter Four

Jack was waiting in his hotel room for a call from Caputo when the lazy morning silence was interrupted by someone knocking on his door.

"Hang on, hang on," he mumbled as he walked over and looked through the peep hole. "Well, what do you know," he said as he pulled the door open to greet Sandy Ryan.

"Good morning, Jack. Hope I didn't interrupt anything."

"At this hour! What could you interrupt?" he motioned for her to come in. "For that matter, at my age you wouldn't be interrupting anything at any hour."

She smiled and entered the room.

"What are your plans for the day? You mentioned yesterday that your were postponing your trip home. Are you still planning to stay for a while?"

Jack nodded "Yeah, this bombing has piqued my curiosity. I'm not in the way, am I?"

"No, as a matter of fact, I was hoping you'd stick around."

"Yeah, but I'm a retired old beat cop. Some of the boys at your headquarters might not be as enthusiastic as you."

"Well, you'd be surprised how much the guys at the office know about you. Apparently, you're a bit of a legend. The people in New York talk about you like you're still working active cases for the NYPD."

"Well, I do lend a hand every now and then," Jack admitted.

"What was it, twenty-seven years on the force, twenty as a gold shield, and not one unsolved case? You cracked them all! Who the hell ever heard of such a thing? You're like the John Edwards of cops. You have a gift, Jack. You stroll around here like some old guy looking for the latest sports section and, within fifteen minutes on site, you've eliminated accident and helped point us in, what I think, is the right direction. Unbelievable!"

"Yeah, well a lot of credit goes to that little lady at the airport, Mrs. Thompson. You would have come to the same conclusion."

"Maybe. But you figured out the terrorist placement and you found the truck."

"Well, we actually found the truck."

"It was you, Jack, and that's why I'm asking you to stick around for a few days and help us set this one straight. I've talked to my boss, he's approved it, and the government's going to pick up the tab. They have a discretionary fund for just such an occasion."

Kane rubbed his hand through his hair and took a deep breath. "Discretionary fund? Just another way to blow my tax money, if you ask me."

"Well, think of it as sort of a tax refund," Sandy grinned.

"Come to think of it, I have been overtaxed these last few years. And there was that summer house property deduction that the IRS denied me last year."

"Well it's time for some payback, Jack."

"And all I have to do is help you find some terrorists, who'll probably slice off my manhood if this backfires and they get their hands on me." Jack frowned.

There was silence for a moment as they both considered the statement.

"I guess there's a downside to everything, isn't there Jack."

"I guess there is." Kane walked to the closet and grabbed his jacket and hat. "Ah, what the hell. It wouldn't be much of a loss. These days I never get a chance to use it any."

Kane locked his room door and the couple started walking toward the elevator.

"I got you authorization to carry a gun. I think I read that your weapon of choice is a Ruger P85 9mm, is that right?"

"You have been doing your homework!"

They reached the elevator, pressed the 'down' button, the doors opened immediately and they stepped in. They were alone.

"Good." she said as she pulled a holstered Ruger from her coat and handed it to Kane. "Stick this on your belt or whatever. Be careful. It's loaded. I have a few boxes of ammunition for you in the car. If you need more..."

Kane took the gun. "If I need more! I haven't shot anybody since Vietnam."

"I know, Jack, and we're not asking you to be Dirty Harry here either. As a matter of fact, you'll probably never have to take it out of the holster. But Jack, these are different times. The rules changed since 9-11."

"Yeah, I know. I spent a lot of days down at Ground Zero; first hoping and praying, then just praying."

A minute or two passed, the elevator stopped, the doors opened and they entered the hotel lobby.

"Hold it Jack, I've got a call." Sandy flipped open her cell phone. "This is Ryan."

She listened and as she did, a puzzled look came over her.

"No kidding? A priest and a crescent moon? We'll be there in half an hour. Don't let anyone touch a thing," she closed the phone and shoved it into her coat. "Come on, Jack. I think there's something we've got to check out."

Traffic was good and they made the trip in twenty minutes. On the way to the Holiday Inn, Sandy explained that it was Caputo who had called and he was standing next to a dead priest who had a gaping hole in the back of his head.

They parked in a no parking zone in front of the hotel and were greeted in the lobby by Caputo.

"We've got to stop meeting this way," Caputo said shaking his friend's hand.

"Ever since we met, bodies have been popping up all over this town. You know, if I didn't know any better, I'd think this city's got a crime problem."

"It is fun, isn't it?"

They took the freight elevator to the fourth floor and a minute or two later were standing in the middle of room 420 looking at, what appeared to be the body of a Roman Catholic priest, who was missing the back half of his skull.

"I'm glad I missed breakfast," was the first thing that Kane said.

"They have an excellent restaurant in this hotel," Caputo said wryly.

Kane waved it off. "No, I'm not very hungry right now."

The investigators were careful not to disturb the crime scene. Ryan checked out the bathroom area while Kane and Caputo moved closer to the deceased.

"So you don't think he's a priest?" said Kane.

"No, I think this was all staged."

"Sandy mentioned a crescent moon?" Kane continued.

"Yup, right here," Caputo pointed to a small tattoo just behind his left ear.

"Muslim?"

"That's what I'm thinking."

"He could have been a convert and just couldn't face the pain of laser tattoo removal." Kane was inches from the body.

"Yeah, well I made a call to the Diocese office. They did a quick search and they don't have a record of any Father Alphonse Capone."

Kane lowered his head and laughed. "You gotta be kidding. Al Capone?"

Caputo laughed too. "That's what the phony ID says and he checked in with that name."

"Yeah, and I'm Bugs Moran," said Kane.

Sandy came out of the bathroom and walked to the other side of the body.

"What a mess," She looked over at Caputo. "I heard you guys talking. So this is Al Capone, huh! Nah, I agree. This is a set up."

Kane looked over at the woman. "I'm glad you concur, but what brought you to that conclusion?"

"Well, for one thing, if he was so repulsed by his lifestyle, why would he want to be found with that piece of porno trash opened on the bed?"

"Maybe he wanted one last look before lights out." Caputo offered.

"Yes, but I hear that if you die suddenly, with a hard on, it doesn't go away." She continued, "It looks like he's as soft as Jell-O."

The two men caught themselves staring at the victim's crotch.

"Where did you hear that?" Kane asked.

"Sounds like an old wive's tail, if you ask me," Caputo mumbled. "I've never seen a dead perp with a woody."

Kane rubbed the side of his nose. "Honestly, I've never paid much attention."

"Well hell, neither have I," Caputo said defensively. "I was just saying…"

Sandy interrupted. "Forget I mentioned the penile rigor mortis. It was just a thought. What's more obvious to me are the shoes. Both laces are untied, and his feet seem to be crammed into them, don't you think?"

"You're right. They are a size or two too small," Kane agreed. "But what got my attention were the bottoms of the shoes."

"What about them?" Caputo asked. "They look normal to me."

"They are normal," Kane said, "and clean. But look at the rug underneath and around the shoes."

Kane touched a finger to the stain. "That's fresh mud. These shoes haven't been in any mud. This guy's been dressed."

Sandy grinned. "And that's why we want you to stick around Jack. As they would say, you've got 'the touch'."

Kane was on a roll. "And these shell casings."

"What about them?" asked Caputo.

"Well, they all appear to be fine except for that one." Kane pointed to one lone casing that was on the floor behind the chair. "I'm thinking that whoever killed this slob shot at the magazine on the bed, from just to his side, trying to make it appear that the victim did the shooting. He was standing a little too far back when he fired one of the rounds and the casing bounced off the good Father Capone's side and landed behind the chair. I'm not a forensics man, but that's my guess."

"Make's sense to me," Caputo agreed.

"All the planning and the killer missed that? Doesn't that seem weird to you?" Sandy questioned.

"Well, it would be a big deal if the killer was really looking to sell this setup to us," Kane said.

"He did a lot of work here, Jack, dressing him, the dirty pictures, the gun shots," Caputo reminded Kane. "It looks to me like he was being pretty specific about everything here."

"I'm not sure what to make of this killer. I really think he missed the tattoo and I think we'll find that this fella here doesn't attend mass every Sunday. I think he's Muslim and if my hunch is correct, he's connected with the plane bombing last night. Probably the driver of the catering truck." Kane thought for a moment. "You know, the shooter may simply be trying to confuse us, to mess with our heads. He may want to make us to over-think this thing."

"If we have a lot of questions and they're all the wrong ones, then we're wasting valuable time." Sandy added.

"And giving him more time to do whatever it is he's going to do," Kane went on.

"This is a diversion?" Caputo wasn't sold. "I don't know guys."

Kane looked around the room. "No, it's not just a diversion. He came here for a reason. And, initially, this guy felt safe in the killer's presence. But once he got what he came for, our friend here was no longer needed."

"He became a liability," Sandy inserted. "After all, he knew who the killer was and probably what he was up to."

Caputo leaned against the desk. "So where do we go from here?"

"We go to breakfast and wait for forensics to do their thing and for the results from the autopsy," he wiped his hands and turned to Caputo. "Do you think you can put a fire under the lab boys and the coroner?"

"Yeah, I think so," Caputo answered.

"Well then people, breakfast is on me, or should I say, the FBI's discretionary fund." He started for the door, followed by Ryan and Caputo.

"Now he wants to eat!" Caputo muttered, as he motioned for the uniform officers to continue their investigation.

Chapter Five

Hakim Abdula looked out the front window of his suburban Pittsburgh home and scanned the street that led to his residence. There was no traffic. He let the curtain drop and turned to his wife.

"Where the hell is he? He should be here by now."

Dana Abdula sat patiently in one of the living room's high back chairs.

"Relax. He said he'd be here soon and he will be. We've waited a long time for this moment. We can afford to wait a few more minutes."

Hakim pushed the drapes aside and looked out again.

"How long have we lived around these swine?"

"Eight years," Dana answered.

"Eight unbearable years. Years of putting up with their looks, their laws, their customs, their hedonism. God how I hate these neighbors, this town, this entire country."

Dana put a hand to her forehead. "We knew, all those years ago, what we were doing and what to expect. And Hakim, you know we've been busy. We've built an amazing network and burrowed deep into this community. You're a respected businessman. To these stupid Americans, you're a real rags-to-riches success. They love hearing about all you've done with nothing."

"Yes, well you and I know I had a little help from al Qaeda, hundreds of thousands of dollars worth of help. It's easy to appear to be a growing business when you have a hidden bankroll." He let the curtain fall again and turned to his wife. "And what of you? You are a successful doctor, you've impeccable credentials, much of which is true, I might add. We were lucky to recruit you in medical school."

"It wasn't hard. I've been behind this cause since the beginning. I'm where I should be."

Hakim walked to the chair and knelt down beside the woman. "I must ask you my dear. Now that the time has almost come for us to strike and then leave all of this behind, what are your thoughts? Have you a change of heart?"

Dana placed a hand on Hakim's cheek. "No my darling. You should know me better by now. My one purpose in life is to kill these infidels. Every time I've helped to deliver one of these pagan bastards, I've wanted to throttle its neck. Allah forgive me, but it's true, every single time. Sometimes it has taken all my energy to conceal my true feelings. No, there is no change of my heart. I'm ready to do what I've waited my whole life to do, and I'm honored that our leader has chosen us to spearhead such an important strike."

"Yes, so am I." Hakim agreed. "Our planning has been meticulous; our training has been, too. We will not, we can not fail."

A car door closed and Hakim returned to the window. "He's here."

Dana stood, walked to the door and opened it. The Ghost was standing on the top step about to ring the doorbell.

"Doctor Abdula?" he grinned.

"Yes…and you are?"

"Let's just say that I am the person that you've been waiting for. Is your husband here, too?"

Hakim stepped from behind the door.

"What do we call you?" Hakim asked.

"My friends call me the Ghost," he said pulling the screen door open. "It's a nickname that I've come to like. It fits too. Now are you going to invite me in?"

The couple stood aside and the Ghost entered their living room.

"I'm sorry I'm late. I'm usually very particular about being on time. I'm afraid this was unavoidable," the Ghost apologized. "With all that I had to do during the past twenty-four hours, who would have thought that I'd get a speeding ticket for doing thirty-five in a twenty-five mile an hour zone, on one of these half-ass small town roads. And the cop was such a cocky son of a bitch. I should have shot the bastard."

Hakim looked alarmed. "But you didn't."

"No, of course I didn't. I grinned, apologized for the mistake and took the ticket."

"Good. We mustn't draw any unnecessary attention," said Dana

"Who would have thought? Thirty-five isn't fast," the Ghost continued. "Ah, but what the hell, I ripped the damned thing up anyway."

"Good," Dana said. "Now, shouldn't we be getting down to business?"

"Absolutely," the Ghost agreed.

"Why don't we go in and sit at the kitchen table?" Hakim suggested. "We can discuss the plan and maybe my good wife will be kind enough to brew us some of her very special coffee."

"Special coffee! Sounds good to me," the Ghost was already walking to the adjacent room.

After a few more minutes of small talk and coffee preparation, the threesome settled in around the Abdula's round oak kitchen table. The Ghost placed the overnight bag he had taken from the hotel on a chair next to where he was seated.

"You mustn't keep us in suspense any longer," Hakim said impatiently. "Do you have the concentrate?"

"Yes, I do."

"May we see it?" Dana asked calmly.

The Ghost hesitated for a moment, looked at the two people and smiled, "Yes, of course."

The couple leaned in a little closer, while the Ghost reached into the bag to retrieve the vials. Carefully and deliberately he placed each one of them on the table in front of the Abdula's. They stared at the containers as if they were gazing at large uncut diamonds.

Dana reached across, picked up one of the cylinders and then took a folded paper from a shirt pocket. She turned the vile until she found a set of numbers. She carefully wrote each digit down next to the numbers that were already there. Then slowly, she compared the two sets of numerals.

"Well? Is this the weapon?" Hakim seemed a little nervous.

Dana gently put the cylinder down and nodded in the affirmative.

"The numbers match. It appears to be the concentrate."

Hakim sighed noticeably. "Well, that's a relief. It's unfortunate that we had to ship the material through such a circuitous route but we couldn't risk losing it. It was important that the delivery team not know what it was they were delivering."

"Yes, well it worked out," the Ghost said. "And they're dead."

The casualness of the remark caught Dana off guard. "Those men were loyal supporters of our movement. Their sacrifice will never be forgotten."

"Nonsense," the Ghost snapped back. "They were duped. They were led to believe that they were on some great mission, when in reality, they were just delivery boys, and expendable ones at that."

Dana's face flushed with anger. "How dare you insinuate that…"

Hakim raised his hand and interrupted his wife. "Dana, we must remember that our friend here isn't one of us. He doesn't share our goals, or even our faith."

"No I don't, and that's why your boss hired me," the Ghost added. "The only thing that I strive for is my success."

Dana sat back in her chair. "And I'll never understand why they retained your services."

The Ghost smiled. "It's really very simple doctor. You see,

I'm absolutely the best in the world at what I do. I'm sure you've heard of Carlos the Jackal?"

The Abdula's both nodded in the affirmative.

"Well, he was good, I am better."

"But how can we expect to succeed if those who help us carry out our fight have no heart, no soul?" Dana asked.

"What I do doesn't require a heart or soul. As a matter of fact, my dear woman, those two assets might get in my way," the Ghost said in a cold and menacing voice. "Now, I'm getting a little tired of this idle banter. You were about to show me your plans."

Dana looked at her husband as if questioning whether to proceed.

"Please don't jerk me around, doctor. You'll find that I don't react well to clients who try to double cross me. Mister Abdula you do want this mission to succeed, don't you?"

"Yes, of course. We haven't come this far and waited this long to fail," he looked to his wife. "We have the utmost confidence in your skills and we apologize for any doubts that we may have expressed."

The Ghost settled back in his chair, pulled a small gun from his coat pocket, un-cocked it and placed the weapon on the table. "Apology accepted. For a moment there I thought we were going to have a little problem."

Suddenly Dana realized how dangerous the situation had become and immediately became compliant. "No, we have no problem. We were about to look at the plans." She lifted an attaché case to the table and unlocked it. She opened the cover and as she began to reach into the case, the Ghost placed a hand on his gun to remind her not to pull out any surprises. She hesitated. "It's all right. I'm just taking out the plans."

"Fine," the Ghost said. "And I'm just reminding you that I'll shoot you and your husband if you're reaching for a gun. I'm very fast, as a matter of fact, you don't want to know how fast I am."

Slowly, the woman withdrew some papers, closed the cover and returned the case to the floor. The Ghost continued to watch with his hand on the gun.

"You do understand, sir, that our plans would have been useless was it not for your success in getting the concentrate."

"Yeah, Yeah." he was growing impatient. "Let's have a look at the damn plans."

Dana turned the folder so that the Ghost could see what was written on the papers. Slowly, silently, the killer read each page and when he was finished he closed the folder and looked up at the Abdulas.

"Well, this should get Homeland Security's attention."

Hakim smiled. "We hope to get the world's attention."

"And you have no qualms about doing this?"

"Not in the least." Dana's reply was cold and definite.

"And which part do you want me to take?" he asked.

"We acknowledge your experience. That is why we think that you should lead our assault," Dana answered. "We have the will and the desire. You, however, have the know-how, the expertise."

The Ghost took the gun from the table and slipped it back into his coat. "You know, when this is over, there are going to be a lot of people out there who are going to hate you."

"They do now," Hakim said.

"I don't care if they hate us, but I do want them to fear us," the doctor said.

"Well, they will that," the Ghost said.

"Their memories are short in this country," Hakim continued. "After our brothers attacked them on September 11th, there was much talk, many threats. But soon, they became complacent and returned to their old ways. 9-11 disappeared from the headlines and was replaced but such important things as Madonna kissing Brittany and who would be the next winner of that disgusting piece of American trash, American Idol. These are a weak people, a selfish, lazy, fat people. They're more concerned with their gluttonous and insatiable appetites. They are ripe to fail and they will, so long as we maintain our resolve."

"Women and children will die," the Ghost reminded.

"The cost of war," the doctor answered.

"How do they describe it when they drop their bombs on our cities and towns? 'Collateral damage' is the term that I think they use," said Hakim. "Please, sir, understand that these plans were prepared with full awareness of what the outcome would be. Do we like killing children? Of course not. Is it necessary for the success of our cause? Absolutely. Will we do it? Without hesitation."

There was silence for a moment.

"Good. Then let's begin," the Ghost said.

Chapter Six

Kane squeezed off a round from the 9mm Ruger Sandy had given him and watched the paper target respond to the hit.

"Looks like you nailed him from here," Caputo observed.

Jack pulled off his head-gear so he could hear Caputo's remarks.

"Yeah, like I can hear you with these things on," he replied.

"I've been looking all over for you. This is the last place I would have expected to find you."

Kane released the clip from the gun and cleared the chamber.

"Well, Sandy gave me this thing and I figured I'd better brush up on how to use it."

Caputo pressed the target retrieval button and the paper silhouette started its journey toward the men.

"I didn't think you were into guns!" Caputo said.

"It goes with the territory, doesn't it? I carried one of these things for a long time. I just haven't fired one recently."

The target stopped and Caputo gave it a quick examination. "Four in the heart and one in the groin. I guess four out of five ain't bad."

"What do you mean four out of five? That's five out of five."

"You meant to shoot him in the nuts?"

"It's what I call my 'Mingo' shot."

"Mingo shot! What the hell is a Mingo shot?"

Kane took a rag from the counter and started to wipe the gun.

"Back in the sixties, when you were, well hell you probably weren't even alive when this happened! Anyway, there was an actor named Ed Ames and he played an Indian named Mingo on TV. Ames was a guest on the Tonight Show one night and they wanted him to demonstrate the use of a tomahawk, so they put this silhouette target up across the stage. He took the tomahawk, steadied himself and threw it right into the target's nuts."

"Intentionally?"

"No, no! Hell, Ames was an actor. He probably never saw a tomahawk before in his life, never mind throw one."

"Well, for an amateur, he sure hit it in a sensitive spot!" Caputo was smiling.

"You can say that again. That kind of shot will slow any man down. That's why, when I'm not trying to kill a guy, I aim at his crotch, and make a soprano out of him."

Caputo put his hand to his groin and winced. "Oh man, my Twinkies hurt just thinking about that."

Kane smiled. "Don't piss me off and you'll have nothing to worry about."

"I'll remember that."

Kane slid the gun into its holster and the two men started for the door.

"Tom, I'd like to review the hotel security tapes."

"No problem. The guys downstairs gave them the once over and didn't come up with anything, but it wouldn't be the first time they missed something."

Sandy Ryan joined Caputo and Kane in the media lab, while they were in the midst of reviewing the footage from the elevator security camera.

"You know Jack, I think you're right!" Caputo said.

"Yeah, I know I'm right." said Kane.

Ryan settled into a chair next to the men. "Would you mind letting me in on your little discovery?"

"I think we're dealing with a big time hired gun." Kane

leaned back in his chair.

Ryan pointed to the picture that was frozen on the lab's video screen. "You mean this guy?"

"Yup." Kane threw a picture on a table next to Sandy. "I think the man up there is the guy in this picture."

Sandy took the picture. "And who would that be?"

"We don't know his real name but they call him the Ghost," Caputo answered.

"This is the Ghost!" she was surprised. "You've got to be kidding."

She looked at the picture again. "You really can't be sure from this picture. It's not all that clear."

"Well it's the best Interpol has," Caputo continued. "As a matter of fact, it's the only thing they have of him."

"Well, that doesn't surprise me. From what I've read about this Ghost, he's as elusive as vapor," again Ryan pointed to the TV screen. "How do you know this is him?"

"It's him, Sandy. Trust me," Kane said definitively.

Caputo leaned toward the young FBI agent. "You see, the good news is, our friend Jack here has seen him."

"What? You're kidding!" Ryan said.

"No, he's very serious. I came face to face with this bad guy on April 30, 1996."

"Boy, he must've left a heck of an impression for you to remember the exact date."

"He left an impression all right, in the form of a 9mm slug in my back. Every time it rains, I think about the son of a bitch."

"He shot you!"

"Well he didn't push the bullet in with his fingers," Kane replied.

"How do you know it was the Ghost?" Sandy asked.

Kane pointed to the picture she was holding. "Look at his right hand."

She did as instructed. "He's missing his pinky finger!"

"Now look at the guy in the elevator." Caputo tapped the operator on the shoulder. "Zoom in on the right hand Frank."

The technician turned a dial on his console and the image moved in on the suspect's hand.

"Well I'll be damned! No pinky finger," Sandy exclaimed.

"How did you know about that, Jack?" Caputo asked.

"He shot me in the back, I shot him in the hand," Jack explained.

"No kidding!" Sandy grinned. "You hit him in the pinky after being shot in the back? That was quite a shot."

"Yeah, well I was aiming at his head."

"Oh."

Kane started to laugh. "I've got to tell you though; it was worth getting shot just to see him dance around the room waving his bloody hand like he was conducting an orchestra."

"You're lucky he didn't finish you off." Caputo noted.

"Yeah, well you'll notice that the missing finger is on his shooting hand. He dropped the gun and was in too much pain to finish the job. He swore a blue steak and took off like a bat out of hell, vowing on the way out the door to one day kill yours truly."

"I didn't know that this Ghost dude was a terrorist?" Caputo asked.

Kane paused for a moment to remember. "No, actually if I remember correctly, he's a mercenary, a hired gun. Literally."

"Someone paid him to kill that guy in the hotel room?" Sandy was still trying to piece it together.

"I think so," Kane added. "I can tell you this much, he works for big bucks."

"How big is big?" asked Caputo.

"Word is he won't leave the house for less than a million and that's only to do a down and dirty job, you know, something quick, easy and close to home."

"Did they ever find his finger?" Sandy was still staring at the monitor, captivated by the image of the man.

"Yes, what was left of it. A 9-millimeter slug can do a real number on a human pinky finger. They got DNA and some decent partials," Kane said. "They got enough to make a case against the guy if they ever get the opportunity."

"What's his history, Jack?" Caputo asked. "What makes this guy so damned special?"

Kane was about to speak but Ryan answered first. "He's been on the scene since the early eighties. They've linked him to the Sadat assassination and the murder of at least three other important political leaders around the world. He seems to have a real knack for killing presidents of small countries."

Kane continued, "But he's not just limited to politicians. He's hit corporate executives and even the bosses of the Galluci and Gambini crime families."

"You've got to be kidding! He's hit the mob! This guy really must have a death wish," Caputo said.

"Sure they've got contracts outstanding on the guy, but even the mob doesn't know his real identity. How do you kill the Ghost if you don't know who the Ghost is?"

"They must know about the missing finger, too."

"Do you know how many men are missing that finger?" Kane asked. "It's mind boggling. You'd be amazed. It would take you a lifetime to kill all the guys with a missing pinky finger. And where do you begin? Never mind the city this guy's from, no one even knows his nationality."

"Someone must know who he is. He gets his assignments and he gets paid," said Caputo.

"Well, you can be sure that he doesn't take checks or advertise in the New York Times." Kane shifted a bit in his chair. "However he arranges it, he's very secretive and very successful."

Sandy turned to Kane. "The Ghost never came back for you."

"That's not to say he won't," said Kane. "He's probably a very patient man. You don't succeed in his line of work without being extremely patient."

"You don't seem worried." Sandy observed.

"I'm not. Next time I'll hit his head."

Chapter Seven

Ranoud Safad sat at his desk in Hakim Abdula's warehouse in Mount Lebanon, Pennsylvania. He had always thought it ironic that their headquarters would be in a town with that name. Officially, Ranoud was executive vice president and in charge of the day-to-day operation of Hakim's lucrative and diverse business. Hakim and Ranoud had been friends for a lifetime. They were almost exactly the same age, separated by just three short months. Ranoud, however, was stronger and more muscular, with the looks of a man ten years younger than Hakim. Over the years, while Abdula had been pushing a pencil, exercising his mind and plotting the plans, Ranoud had been working the docks, learning the trades, lifting the crates and tossing the bodies. One was a general, a strategist, the other a battle hardened front lines warrior. Their devotion and loyalty to each other was unquestioned and total. In many ways, Hakim was more committed to Ranoud, than to his wife. They would kill for each other, and they had.

The door opened and Hakim entered the cavernous building. It was after hours and the two men were alone.

"How goes it, my friend?" Ranoud bellowed.

As Hakim walked closer, Ranoud could see a look of concern on his friend's face.

"It could be better," Hakim replied. "And it could be worse."

Ranoud stood and pulled a side chair over to his desk so his friend could sit down.

"Sit Hakim and tell me all about it."

The men sat at the desk and Ranoud pulled a small bottle and two glasses from his desk drawer.

"I know that our religion frowns upon the use of such a thing, but sometimes, in moments like this, it is a necessary evil, don't you think?" Ranoud asked as he poured two glasses of Makers Mark bourbon. There was no argument from Hakim who took the glass only after it was filled to the top.

Ranoud downed a generous swallow and then asked, "Did you get the concentrate?"

"It was delivered to my house a short time ago."

"Wonderful!" Ranoud replied. "Then why the troubled expression?"

"I'm concerned about our delivery boy."

Ranoud leaned forward in his chair. "What about our delivery boy, Hakim?"

Hakim took a swig of the bourbon and continued, "He's very, very dangerous."

"Isn't that good? Isn't he supposed to be dangerous?"

"He's not one of us, Ranoud. He's not with the cause. He's a mercenary, in it only for the money."

Ranoud leaned back in his chair. "But didn't we know this? Weren't we told that our man would be an expert and a hired gun?"

"Yes, this is what we were told. But I don't trust him. He seems as predictable as old, sweaty dynamite. He likes to kill, Ranoud, and will do so in a heartbeat. I don't think he really cares who he kills."

Safad sat quietly in his chair and stared at the golden-brown liquid in his glass.

"We need him. He has the experience and expertise, but I think that, in the long run, he jeopardizes the mission and our cause," Hakim continued.

"Doesn't our leader know his background?" Ranoud asked.

"Yes, of course he does."

"What were his instructions?"

"Use him as we see fit."

"And then?"

Hakim thought for a moment. "There were no other instructions. It was left pretty much open-ended."

Ranoud put down the glass, smiled and clapped his hands. "Well then there is no problem, my brother. We'll watch him like a hawk, use him to our benefit, and then cut his throat."

Hakim looked relieved. "Yes, of course, but we'll have to be careful. This one has eyes in the back of his head and reads minds."

"But when cut, his blood is as red as yours or mine," Ranoud finished. "Relax Hakim. I'll do it myself. Have I ever failed you in the past?"

"No, my friend."

"And I won't fail you now." Ranoud took the glass again and raised it to his lips. "The moment the mission is completed and we are in the clear; I'll slice him from ear to ear. He will die quickly and quietly." He took another big drink.

Hakim was smiling now. "I feel better Ranoud. If anyone can take him out it is you."

Ranoud smiled displaying his trademark gold front tooth. The two men finished their drinks at the same time, almost as if it were a toast.

"So what of the plans, Hakim?" Ranoud asked as he put his glass back into his desk drawer.

"Not now, Ranoud. This is not the time or place. The walls have ears. We'll meet at my cabin in Wheeling tomorrow evening."

"I like Oglebay Park," Ranoud said approvingly. "Will everyone be there?"

"Everyone who needs to be there will be there. Plan on staying the night," Hakim said as he stood, preparing to take his leave.

"Will our delivery boy friend be there?"

"Yes, he'll be there,"

"And does he have a name?"

"No one seems to know his real name. He calls himself the Ghost."

"The Ghost!" Ranoud seemed to be examining the name. "Interesting name, the Ghost."

Ranoud stood and put his hand on his friend's shoulder. "Well… we'll make him one soon enough."

Hakim chortled a bit. "I must be going. I'm meeting Dana downtown. We're having a celebratory dinner, in anticipation of our successful mission."

"Good and please give the lovely woman my warmest regards," Ranoud said as they both started to walk towards the door.

"Ranoud…you know that there is a downside to all of this. There is no guarantee that we'll survive the attack."

"Dying in the name of Allah is not a downside, it is a dream. To spend eternity in heaven is what we are all living for."

"Yes, it is. My sentiments exactly. I just thought that I should remind you so there is no confusion."

"You more than anyone in this world should know how I feel about our cause and how far I'm willing to go to ensure its success," Ranoud said to his friend.

The two men finished the walk to the door and Hakim pulled it open.

"Why don't you close this place up and join us for dinner, Ranoud?" Hakim suggested.

Ranoud thought for a moment. "I wouldn't want to intrude, my friend. I would think that Dana is expecting a quiet night alone with her husband."

"Well then won't she be surprised,"

"You're sure, Hakim?"

"Consider it an order. Besides, Dana will be delighted to see you."

"And I'll be delighted to see her, too," Ranoud added as he pulled a master switch near the door and the lights in the building went out.

"No talk of business tonight," said Hakim

They were now outside of the building and Ranoud was locking the door. "Absolutely not. Tonight we laugh and talk of old times."

The two old friends walked to Hakim's car, got in and a moment later drove out of the dark parking lot. It wasn't until the vehicle had driven out of site that a man appeared from the darkened shadows, stepped carefully onto a narrow ledge that ran along the perimeter of the second floor of the warehouse building, moved to a sub-roof and then dropped to the parking lot pavement. His silhouette, illuminated by a single Halogen light, could be seen hurrying out of the lot to a parked car across the street from the warehouse. He opened the driver's side door and slid in behind the wheel. The guy took a moment to review, in his mind, what he had just seen and heard. While he sat there, he pulled a pair of leather gloves from his hands, four fingers and a thumb from one, and then three fingers and a thumb from the other. The Ghost really wasn't surprised. He had never expected their loyalty. Tonight's meeting had simply confirmed his beliefs.

Chapter Eight

Jack Kane and Sandy Ryan were dining, but not at one of Pittsburgh's high-end eating establishments. The crowd that patronized the Black Crow was more blue uniform than blue blood. But it was a clean little restaurant that served good food and catered to the people who worked at the station house around the corner. It was always busy. Kane and Ryan were seated at a corner booth in the back of the dining room.

"What do we know?" Kane asked. "We know that there were four men in the initial attack at the airport. We know that three were killed on site and the other escaped to the hotel."

Sandy continued. "We know that he met your friend with the missing pinky in his hotel room and that his services were permanently terminated shortly after that little soiree. And that's where the list seems to come to an abrupt end."

"Well…not really," he corrected the younger agent. "We know that he walked out with the bag our vic carried into the hotel. The Ghost went there for that bag. We also know that he took the dead man's car! I'm not really sure why he did that."

"Maybe he took a cab to the hotel." Sandy suggested.

"Maybe. We should check all the cab companies in the area and see if any of the drivers can recognize the fingerless freak."

"Good idea, Jack."

Kane rubbed his eyes. It had been a long day. What was to have been a short one-night stay in the Burgh was turning into another long, complicated and dangerous case. He was silent for a moment. He looked tired.

Sandy could see his exhaustion. "Jack, you look beat. I'm sorry I dragged you into this mess."

Kane waved her off. "Don't be ridiculous. What would I have done if I went home? I would have moped around and thought about this case. I would have wanted to be here, to be in the game. I was hoping someone would ask me to stay. I want to be here, Sandy. I just wish I was twenty years younger and didn't burn out as fast as I do now."

Sandy smiled. "It's not your age Jack. I'm tired too. Heck, we're all beat.

She paused and then continued, "Who would have thought that you'd have a history with this guy, this sick bastard who calls himself the Ghost? Your being involved with this case is a bonus for us."

Kane was scribbling on his place mat. "It's not really much of a history. He shot me and I shot him back."

Sandy leaned forward towards Kane, "But what led up to that Jack? What led up to the shooting?"

"Do you remember what else happened on April 30th, 1996?" Kane asked.

Sandy thought for a moment. "Wait a second, wasn't there an assassination attempt on some head of state?"

Kane nodded in the affirmative. "Yup. A group of Northern Ireland terrorists tried to kill the Prime Minister of Ireland while he was in New York City to speak before the UN General Assembly."

Sandy's eyes widened. "You worked that case?"

"I was assigned to liaison with the PM's security people. At the time I was one of the city's highest ranking detectives," Jack explained. "I was honored to get that assignment."

Sandy nodded in agreement. "Anyone would be."

"Yeah, but with a name like John Patrick Kane, working the security detail that guarded the Prime Minister of the Emerald Isle, well all my ancestors were watching me, if you know what I mean," Kane said as he gestured towards the heavens.

"Ryan is my ex-husband's name," Sandy said.

"Oh, then how could you know?"

"My maiden name is Powers. I come from a long line of Irish cops."

"Well then I guess you do know." Kane smiled. "Anyway, the initial part of the trip went without a hitch. We met his plane at Kennedy, he did his meet and greet and we did the motorcade to Manhattan and met the President at the United Nations. There was another press conference at the UN building and then he went in and gave his speech. After that was over, we piled into the limos and headed for the embassy. There weren't even any demonstrators along the way. It was a quiet, uneventful ride. We pulled up in

front of the Irish Embassy and security got out to do a once-over. We're not out of the car two minutes and I see this uniformed cop strolling toward us with a package in his hand. I pulled my gun and told him to stop and put down the package."

"There weren't supposed to be any other cops there, right?" Sandy assessed.

"That's right."

"So what did he do?"

"What would you do with a loaded gun pointed at your chest? Carefully, he put the package down and stepped away. Being the curious fool that I am, I walked over to the damned thing and looked inside."

"What was it?" she asked.

"A sandwich and an apple."

"You mean he was legit!"

"No. I mean that while I was examining his lunch, he had moved nearer to the limousine."

"But the door was closed, right?"

"Ah, well, that's where we fell down," Kane said, as if it were painful to remember the memory. "It was still open. We hadn't been there sixty seconds."

"Oh boy." Sandy knew where it was going.

"All of a sudden, I heard a gun going off. I looked over and the mystery cop had just shot a security officer who was standing next to the limo. I yelled for the shooter to drop the weapon and I saw him turn toward me! I did an about face in an attempt to jump out of his line of fire and wham-o, suddenly I was on my face with this incredible pain in my back."

"What about the PM? Wasn't he sitting in a limo with an open door?"

"Yes, but when the assassin turned toward me, one of the aides in the limo pulled the door closed and threw the security locks. From that point on he was safe. The car was completely bulletproofed. When the killer heard the locks engage, he became furious."

"I'll bet."

"He was getting ready to shoot me again but I fired first…."

"And hit him in the hand," she finished the sentence.

"And that's when he started to dance, and to curse, and to vow that he'd find out who I was, and kill me."

"Do you think he did?"

"What? Kill me?" Kane smiled.

"No, don't be silly. Do you think he found out who you were?"

Kane took the napkin from the table and placed it in his lap. "I know he did. You see my picture was plastered all over the papers. I was a celebrity. One morning I got a letter with a newspaper clipping that had my picture in it. My face was circled and x'ed out. The note that accompanied the picture was short and not so sweet. It said 'Next time, Jack, you're dead.'"

Kane paused as if to consider the threat again.

"Obviously he's a man of few words. I later learned from Interpol that it was the notorious Ghost who had tried to kill the Prime Minister and me."

Sandy sipped some water. "And now you meet again."

"Just lucky, I guess."

"What happened after that?"

Jack sighed and then answered. "I was done on the job. Not because I screwed up. Like I said, in the city's eyes I was a hero. I was through because of the disability."

"You look okay to me," she observed.

"Yeah, well it took ten months of treatment and therapy to get me back on my feet. Doctors said the bullet just missed my spinal cord. It still hurts when it rains."

"You're lucky to be alive."

"I'd say that given the choice of the back or pinky, I'd have picked the pinky." Kane smiled.

"And he just disappeared?"

"Like a ghost. When I was recuperating, I did a lot of research on the guy, or should I say as much as you can when all you have is a phony name. He's wanted all over the world and he's a master of disguise. He can look like a young jogger or an elderly old man. He can blow you up, shoot you between the eyes from a football field away, or jam a gun into your ribs and kill you up close and personal. He's not fussy about who he kills. He's done women and children, handicapped and the elderly. He's blown up a school bus, cut the throat of a crippled man in a wheelchair and pushed a butcher knife into a pregnant woman's stomach. He's about as close to the devil as you'll get on this earth."

"All that and they've got zilch."

"They don't even know his nationality. They think he's American. But then again he could be Canadian, or English and good with accents." he paused. "Well, you know where I'm going."

"What do you think?"

"I'm as lost as the next guy. Hell, he could be anybody from anywhere. I do know that if he's involved in this, then it's big and we've got to stop it."

They both sat quietly for a moment. Then Jack asked, "Anything big scheduled to happen here in the near future?"

Sandy thought for a moment. "The President is going to be in town this Friday and Saturday."

"What for?" Jack inquired.

"Well, actually he's doing two major things. First, he's addressing the National Conference of Christians and Jews on Friday afternoon. They're holding a conference at the David L. Lawrence convention center. Then he's scheduled a dinner meeting with Israeli Prime Minister Sharon, who's in Pittsburgh to address the same convention on Saturday."

"Oh yeah," Kane remembered. "I read about this little trip. He's making a big mid-East policy speech, right?"

"That's right. I understand he's proposing a new Arab Israeli peace initiative

"Any idea where the President and the Prime Minister are holding their little confab?"

"Word around the office is that they'll be cruising the Three Rivers."

"What do you mean?"

"It's being held on one of the Gateway Clipper river boats."

Kane shook his head. "They're meeting on a boat in the middle of a river! That's going to be a security nightmare. They'll be sitting ducks out there. They can be hit from shore, by water or from the air. Why hasn't the Secret Service nixed that idea?"

"I've heard that this president has a mind of his own. You can suggest, you can propose, you can recommend, but you can't order him to do anything he doesn't want to do. I mean, Jack, he is the President of the United States, for crying out loud."

"So was John Kennedy and look where it got him. Well, I'll bet you my retirement that our friend, the Ghost, is in town to ruin the President's visit."

"You think they'll try to assassinate him?" Sandy asked.

"Maybe it'll be a two for one, the President and the Prime Minister."

Sandy pulled a cell phone from her coat pocket. "I've got to tell my boss. He's got to talk to the people over at the Treasury. The Secret Service has got to shut this trip down."

"Good luck!" Jack offered.

"What do you mean?" Sandy was just about to dial a number.

"Don't get me wrong. I agree. You've got to tell the guys upstairs. But it's not going to stop this trip."

"Why do you say that?"

"Remember how he was after 9-11? The site was still on fire and he was up on the stump with a bullhorn. They weren't sure what was going to happen next, or when, and he was throwing the first pitch out at the World Series over at Yankee Stadium. Talk about walking around with a bull's-eye on your chest." Jack rubbed his eyes and continued. "No. This president of ours is a good old boy from Texas. I don't think he believes in backing down from a fight. We'd better plan on stopping the bad guys before they get their chance to attack."

"Sorry I'm late." It was Caputo. "Something very interesting came up."

He slid into the booth next to Sandy.

"No big thing," said Sandy. "We haven't even ordered yet."

"What's up?" Kane asked.

Caputo placed a manila envelope on the table and pulled out a set of black and white pictures. "That 'be on the lookout' we placed for a man with a missing pinky finger, well we got lucky."

Caputo turned the picture toward Kane.

"Well, well, well! What do we have here?" Kane said as he leaned closer to the photographs.

"What you're looking at are stills taken from a police cruiser video, shot earlier today, in Bethel Park, Pennsylvania. It would appear that this Ghost character has a heavy foot." Caputo said.

"Obviously he was using a phony license. What about the registration?"

"Turns out the car was a rental. The name he used on the fake license was on the temporary registration as an approved driver. Initially, when they ran it on site, nothing came up. When we did some investigating, we found out that he was using the name of a real, living person, it's just that he wasn't that person."

"Tommy, my boy, it's a start." Kane smiled. "We know he's still in town and he's still driving the CRV."

Sandy turned the pictures in her direction. "He looks like Joe Average. He could be the local Boy Scout leader."

"Or parish priest, or traveling salesman. He's a chameleon," said Kane.

Caputo continued. "The questions are who is he working with and why is he here?"

"We can't answer the first question, although we have our suspicions," Sandy answered. "We do think we know why he's in town."

She then spent the next few minutes telling her colleague about the President's visit and his itinerary, and their theory. When she was finished, the three of them sat quietly again, absorbing the information and trying to decide what would be their next move.

"We're really in a strange situation here." Sandy was the first to break the silence. "Considering the circumstances, we have a lot of information. But when you really get down to it, we don't know squat about what's going on here and how it's going to happen."

"Well, I wouldn't throw in the towel just yet," Kane answered. "I know I've described this Ghost character as being elusive, almost superhuman. But he's not. Remember, when I shot him back in 1996, he bled like a stuck pig and squealed like one, too. He's already made a bunch of mistakes. Let us not forget the security tapes in the hotel and the speeding ticket. I'm sure he's very good at what he does, but I'm convinced that we can nail this guy."

"Okay Jack, I'm with you," Caputo agreed. "The guy's human and we can get him. What's next? Where do we go from here?"

"We have something to eat and then we get some rest," Kane said as he picked up a menu. "We're all tired and things will appear fresher to us in the morning."

"But don't you think that time is of the essence?" Sandy asked.

"Absolutely," Kane answered. "But I also think the bad guys will be sleeping tonight and they'll be rested when they start their day in the morning. I think we should be, too."

That answer was good enough for Caputo and Ryan. A moment later the waitress appeared.

* * * *

It was 7:30 AM and Sandy was surprised to find her consultant friend, Jack Kane, already at his desk, pouring through a pile of overnight reports and a stack of computer printouts. He looked tired and was wearing the same clothes he had worn the day before.

She paused in front of his desk. "What happened to the lecture about getting a good night's sleep and being rested in the morning?"

"I didn't sleep very well. It happens a lot at my age."

"Yeah right," she wasn't accepting his answer. "You spent the night thinking about this case, just like I did, and Tom probably did, too. You send us home and you spend the night in here! No wonder you're not married anymore."

Kane lowered his head, as if wounded by the remark. Sandy immediately realized her mistake.

"I'm sorry, Jack. I didn't mean it that way."

Jack looked up again and smiled. "No, you're right. No woman could put up with me. I'm one hundred percent cop. Even in retirement it consumes me. My wife was the best. No one tried harder than her to make it work. It's just that I was hardly ever home and when I was, I brought the damned job home with me."

"Hey Jack, no man will put up with me either," Sandy said, still trying to correct her verbal faux pas. "This 'cop' thing ruins relationships."

The conversation was becoming awkward and it was a good thing that Tom entered the room, and the conversation, when he did. He could see the strained look on Sandy's face.

"You look like its prom night and you totaled your parent's car," he said to her.

"No, I just finished having fillet of foot," Sandy answered.

"Oh!" Tom knew that a change of topic was in order. He turned to Jack. "You're in town a couple of days and you've already made the front page."

Tom threw the morning newspaper on the desk in front of Jack and pointed to a picture of the three of them talking at the airport.

"I don't remember seeing a photographer!" Sandy sounded surprised.

"Well, he was there," Tom said. "Then again, it could have been taken by anyone in the gate area who had a camera."

Jack adjusted his glasses for a clearer examination of the picture. "No photo byline. A stringer probably took it." He leaned back in his chair, "Just what I need, publicity. Like I didn't get enough the last time I was in this city."

* * * *

The man with the missing finger gave the front page picture one more look. "How lucky can I get? I'm not even looking for you, Mr. Kane, and you fall into my lap. Well, this time you won't crawl away. The next time we meet will be the last time you meet anybody, and it will be soon, Jack, very soon."

He folded the newspaper, took a lighter from his pocket, flicked it and held the flame to the end pages, until the burn took hold. Then he tossed it onto the front seat of his CRV, stepped back a safe distance and watched as the fire grew in intensity. A few minutes later the car exploded in a fiery ball.

"Well, so much for that," he said out loud to himself. He walked over to a brand new Jeep, got in and drove away.

Chapter Nine

Hakim's cabin sat on the fringe of picturesque Oglebay Park in Wheeling, West Virginia. To someone unfamiliar with the area, Wheeling may seem to be a world away from Pittsburgh, but in reality it's a short fifty-mile drive from the heart of the steel city. Hakim prided himself in making the trip in less than an hour. He called it a cabin but it was actually much more. Most people would say it was palatial, ostentatious and lavish. Usually cabins are one or two rooms. This cabin had three bathrooms and six bedrooms. There was a large swimming pool in the backyard and the view from the living room was an unobstructed panorama of twenty rolling miles of West Virginia wilderness. This cabin had cost Hakim one point two million dollars. But what's money when you've got an unlimited source. He was supposed to look like a self made man living the American dream and he was doing a damn good job of it.

Hakim and Dana spent the early part of the evening greeting their guests. Of course Ranoud had been the first to arrive. Fifteen or twenty minutes later Khalil Rasheed walked through the door. He was a tall, well built man and a passionate follower of the cause. He had been with the team since its inception, eight years earlier, and was considered by all to be a facilitator, a man who got things done, sometimes impossible things. Mohammed Khan, another team leader, arrived minutes later. He was a newer but nonetheless trusted associate. He had arrived in the United States by way of Canada and was here illegally. Hakim had furnished him with false documentation, a fictitious history and a well paying job. Unlike most illegals, he was more like a well-trained and highly educated spy. His English was impeccable, better than most on the team. He had a vast knowledge of weapons and he knew things about America that many Americans didn't know. The only thing greater than his knowledge of the United States was his hatred for the country. He was still fighting the crusades and every non-Muslim American was an enemy and potential target. Tonight he was pumped, excited that their attack was about to begin. Abu Mirad, the last of the team leaders, pulled into the driveway fifteen minutes after Khan. The only person missing was the Ghost. Hakim waited a while longer for him to arrive.

"Aren't we all here?" Khan asked.

"There's one more," Hakim said softly.

"One more! But who?" Mirad questioned.

Dana turned from the front window and walked closer to the assembled group.

"There's a new arrival. Our leader sent him to us just this week," she answered.

"Do we know this man?" Khan continued.

"Not really." said Hakim. "All I know is that he had certain necessary skills and that he was sent by our leader."

"Well what's his…"

Hakim finished Khan's question, "… name? I can't tell you this."

"But you know us, Hakim," Mirad said. "If you can trust us with your life, can't you trust us with his name?"

"That's not the point," Hakim replied. "I don't know his real name. I doubt if anyone in our organization does. All I know is that he is known as the Ghost."

Khan recognized the name immediately.

"My God! He is part of our team?" There was a tone of fear in his question.

"You know of him?" asked Ranoud.

"I know that he's a hired gun," Khan answered. "He'll work for anyone, as long as they can pay his fee, which is usually astronomical. He has no morals, no beliefs, no values."

By now everyone in the room was facing Khan.

"He has killed Arab and Jew alike, heads of state and lowly operatives. He has no country, no loyalty. I can't believe that our leader would bring him into the fold!"

"Believe it." Everyone in the room turned to see the Ghost standing in the doorway.

"We didn't hear you arrive," Hakim said to the mercenary.

"No kidding," the Ghost said sarcastically. He walked over to Khan and stopped just inches from his face. "It just so happens, my dear boy, that I do have a country, and a name, and a mother and father, and a loyalty, none of which is your business." Now he had his hand in his pocket. "Do you have a problem with that?"

Khan, a man who was unaccustomed to being afraid of any man, was suddenly aware that the wrong answer could be his last.

"No…I do not."

The Ghost held his position. "Well, then say you sorry."

"What?" Khan was caught off guard.

The Ghost inched even closer. "Are you deaf? I said, say you're sorry."

Khan paused. He didn't want to, but he knew he had to. "I'm sorry."

The Ghost paused, as if considering the answer and then smiled broadly. "Good. That's better. Now we can all be friends."

Hakim closed the living room door. "Yes, well I would think that introductions are in order."

The Ghost turned to the host "None needed. I know everything there is to know about each one of you, everything. And I'm quite sure you all know me. Let's get down to business. I have things to do."

"But aren't you staying the night?" asked Dana.

"Here? With you? I don't think so," said the Ghost.

"Well then, let's get started," Ranoud said.

The group moved to a large oval table in the dining area and sat down.

"I've asked you, the leaders of our team, to meet here tonight, to review and discuss our plan of attack. You've all been very patient and I deeply appreciate your being so." Hakim began.

"9-11 was a beginning, a good beginning. But compared with what we have planned, it was a skirmish."

Everyone's eyes widened with interest, everyone, that is, except the Ghost.

"These Americans have a great deal, but two things they don't have are patience and character. They're soft and have no will to fight. They're not the same people who won the Second World War. These people are products of the sixties and the seventies, the weak pot smoking fools who have no stamina. And, the younger ones? Well, they are their spineless, materialistic offspring."

He picked up a glass that was in front of him, took a sip of water and continued. "Never mind being Christians or Jews, most Americans have no real faith at all. They have no God. Their god is excess. They're hollow people. They're lost and empty souls who have fouled our world and must be eliminated for the betterment of mankind. Allah and our great leader have given us the responsibility to begin that process."

He paused and panned the room for reaction. Everyone seemed in agreement. Everyone, that is, except the Ghost. He sat across the table quietly shaking his head.

"You have a problem with something I've said?" There was anger in Hakim's voice.

"What difference does it make what I think?" the Ghost said.

"To some of us it may make a great deal of difference."

The Ghost leaned closer to the table. "All right. Remember, you asked."

He paused a moment and then continued.

"You see, Mr. Abdula, I've never been one to underestimate my opponent. You trivialize the Americans and make them appear stupid and weak."

"They are!" Hakim interrupted.

"Well, if this is how you're going to approach this mission then I think I should bow out now, before it's too late."

"What makes you think it's not too late now?" Ranoud asked.

The Ghost smiled. "You don't know me very well, Mr. Safad. For that matter, you don't know me at all. I've managed to stay alive and make a good living by being one step ahead of the game. Do you really think that I couldn't walk away right now? Granted, if push came to shove, I might be leaving a room full of bodies behind me, but trust me, I could go and you couldn't stop me."

The room was silent. The Ghost continued, "But I didn't come all this way, on your leader's behalf, to walk away now. I promised him that I would pull this off and I'm going to do just that. If anyone doesn't complete this mission, it will be one of you, not me."

He directed his attention to Hakim again. "Never underestimate your opponent. These Americans have great resources and a resolve of steel when threatened. If we don't execute this mission precisely as planned, it will fail and many, if not all, of us will die. Now, I don't know about you people, but I don't anticipate an afterlife surrounded by seventy Vestal virgins. Hell, with my history, I'll be lucky to spend eternity with one wretched street whore. That being said, I'm not looking to step into the great unknown any time soon. If any of you plan on making this mission an exercise in martyrdom then tell me now and I'll be on my way."

Again there was silence.

The Ghost looked around the table. He could see the distrust in each man's face. He had said what they didn't want to hear.

"My friend, Hakim, knows these people," Khalil said. "No one has a better sense of who they are and what we're up against."

"Well, if you believe what he just said, then you're about to meet Allah. In order to beat the Americans, you're going to have to think like Americans."

"And you know how they think?" Khan said, with a mocking tone in his voice.

"Yes I do," the Ghost replied.

"And how can that be?"

"Because I am one." he snapped back quickly.

The group took a moment to absorb what he had just said.

"What about your English accent?" Dana asked.

"What about it?" the Ghost answered quickly. "Would you like to hear my French accent?" he said with a heavy French accent. "How about German?" He spoke like a Bavarian native. "Or maybe you're partial to Russian,". he continued, sounding every bit as Russian as Vladimir Putin.

"Impressive," Hakim said.

"Not really," said the Ghost. "They're meaningless unless you know their mannerisms, each individual language fluently and their way of life.

"And you do?" Khan asked.

"Yes I do," the Ghost said contemptuously. "It's every bit as important to me as my knowledge of weapons and explosives."

"So, what do you suggest, Mister, whatever your name is?" Hakim went on.

"I would suggest a healthy respect for the enemy."

"That will be hard to do," Ranoud interjected.

"You'd better make it happen, my friend, or this mission is doomed. It's okay to hate these people, but never take them for granted. They may be morally bankrupt, but they're not stupid. They're like a lot of animals. When frightened they'll run and run fast, but when cornered, with no place to go, they'll strike back and possibly eat you alive."

Khan asked the two questions that were going through each of their minds. "If you're one of them, why are you doing this, and why should we trust you?"

The Ghost turned directly to Khan. His gaze was piercing and cold. "Why I'm doing this is my business. Suffice it to say that your leader trusts me. Do you dare question him?"

Khan looked away and to the rest of the group. "Of course not. I'd follow him to the grave."

"Well, let's just hope that doesn't happen anytime soon," said the Ghost.

The Ghost turned his attention again to the entire group. "I was sent here to help make this mission a success. I have skills and knowledge that none of you have. That being said, I want you to know that each of you is an integral part of the whole operation. I'm not here to bully you or to take control of the organization. I'm here to facilitate." He looked to Hakim. "Mr. Abdula, you've worked long and hard planning this operation. You've sold the greatest terror organization in the world on its viability. We believe in your goals. But don't underestimate the Americans."

"I've lived among them for years. I may be passionate about my disdain for these people, but I know they're dangerous." Hakim said in his defense. "You may have judged me too soon, my friend. You'll find that my plan is meticulous and well thought out. You'll see that I've always assumed that they're on to us. Each part of my plan has a work around, in the event that something goes wrong. I can see where you may mistake my enthusiasm for our cause for unbridled fanaticism. But don't. With the exception of yourself, I know each man in this room and they know me. We are connected by our faith and common history. They know where I'm coming from, my friend. The only unknown in the room is you. Now, be assured that we're glad you are here. We trust and love our leader and know that he would never send us someone who would interfere with our work." This time it was Hakim who leaned toward the Ghost with a dangerous look. "Just remember what I said. Every phase of this operation has a back up. If something or someone gets in our way, they will be removed, permanently."

"Yes, well good" the Ghost said. "We're all on the same page then aren't we? And, you don't trust me, and I don't trust you. I find working under those conditions healthy, don't you? We'll both be sharper now, don't you think? And, of course if one of us screws up, the other one will kill him. It's refreshing, really. And if everyone does their job, you'll have your success, I'll be on my way, and life will be good. Now, what's the plan?"

Hakim stared at the Ghost for a second. It was the first time since they'd met that he had actually considered reaching into his jacket sleeve, for his derringer, and shooting the stranger on the spot. In his mind, he even visualized the gun going off and the red spot appearing in the center of the man's forehead. But it was only a passing thought and he knew that he'd need him alive, for the moment. When the mission was over, this arrogant mercenary would be finished too.

"The plan?" the Ghost prodded again.

Hakim took a deep breath and began. "Yes, well as you all know, I've managed to build a successful and somewhat diversified business, thanks of course to the support of our leader and his constant infusion of funds. Most of our business deals with the transport of fuel, chemicals and propane. I've also managed to establish an impeccable reputation within the community. I've been a member of the Rotary and been the president of the Chamber of Commerce. I'm even the leader of Arabs for America." he laughed. The others at the table seemed amused too, with the exception, of course, of the Ghost. "I'm trusted. Why, even after our brothers attacked New York and Washington on September 11th, no one ever questioned me? I was above reproach. Outwardly, my wife and I grieved with our neighbors and the community, but privately we rejoiced and celebrated our success, didn't we Dana?" he said to his wife.

"Yes, my darling," she agreed.

"We have built a strong operation and each of our drivers, every single one of them, is a soldier in our organization. Oh, you may look at our books and see names such as DiNunzio and Lopez, but they are covers. All of our men were sent here to be trained for this week's attack. They may look Italian or Hispanic, but they are Arab and believers. They are all willing to sacrifice themselves for the success of our effort, and unfortunately, if all goes as planned, most of them will have to do just that."

Hakim stood and walked to a map of the city of Pittsburgh that was on an easel next to the table.

"When our cell was formed and inserted into this country, our mission was to lie low until a strong target of opportunity presented itself. One of our strengths is our patience. We've stayed here for years, waiting for just the right opportunity. This coming Friday the President of the United States and that vile pig, Ariel Sharon, will be in this city. Not Jerusalem or Tel Aviv, but Pittsburgh, Pennsylvania. Our moment has finally come. With one devastating attack, we will eliminate two of our most hated enemies, kill hundreds if not thousands of their followers, and send a resounding message to the rest of the world." He pointed to the map. "Look at this city. It was made for what we have planned. The main business area is bordered by water, the Allegheny River to the north and the Monongahela River to its south. There are only a handful of major arteries in and out of town. From the west, the main access is the Fort Pitt tunnels and bridge, from the south you would use the Liberty Tubes and bridge and maybe a handful of smaller spans. If you entered Pittsburgh from the east, you would most likely use the Parkway and the most common access from the north would be the Parkway north route 279. The President is scheduled to arrive in the city at 1PM. Sharon will be here even earlier at around 11AM. Both men are staying in a downtown hotel. Our plan is to completely block access in and out of town at the height of the Friday afternoon rush hour. How will we do that?" He took another sip of water and continued, "Each access, inbound and outbound, will be blocked, at precisely the same time, by fully loaded propane tanker trucks. Moments later, and again, at the exact same time, these fully loaded trucks will be detonated by their drivers. The explosions alone should kill hundreds and destroy all access in and out of the city. It will create a panic environment and cause enormous confusion for the authorities."

Abu Mirad, who had been quiet, interrupted his friend. "One question, Hakim. Three inbound routes go through tunnels. To the west there's the Fort Pitt Tunnels, to the east, there's the Squirrel Hill tunnels and if you enter or leave the city from the south you must use the Liberty Tubes. Aren't trucks with hazardous fuels prohibited from using tunnels?"

Hakim smiled. "Yes, Abu, and intentionally blowing up trucks is prohibited too."

Abu sat back in his chair looking a bit sheepish and wishing he had remained quiet. Hakim put his hand, reassuringly, on his friend's forearm. "It's a good question, my friend. I want you to think about what it is we're about to do. If we overlook something, it's you people in this room who might catch it, before we actually make the mistake." The smile disappeared and, this time, he was serious when he addressed the question. "There are no gates at the entrance to the tunnels, only flashing lights. Yes, there is a good possibility, no make that a good probability, that they will light those warning signals, as our trucks near the tunnels. Those lights will be ignored. As a matter of fact, even though our trucks will be strategically placed so that they are in the tunnels or at their detonation points at precisely the right time, there is no guarantee that something won't go wrong and the highway won't be obstructed."

The Ghost simply sat across from Hakim and listened. Hakim continued, "These tankers, fully loaded are incredibly heavy, they weigh many several tons. The tractors that pull them are equipped with one of the most powerful truck engines in the world. We have reinforced the front end of each rig so that they are now, quite literally, battering rams. If they are stopped short of their target destination and time is running out, their orders will be for them to plow the rest of the way."

"What if they're a couple of hundred yards away? That's a lot of cars to move." Khalil Rasheed said.

"Yes, well we think these trucks and their drivers are up to the task. At the very least, they will get as close as they can before the explosion. This part of the plan has been my direct responsibility. I have trained these people and built these trucks. They are as good as you can get for this mission. If they fail then their failure is mine and I will accept full responsibility. No one else in this room will be blamed." Hakim paused and then continued, "But they will not fail. They have been trained and trained well. These drivers are special people, the cream of our crop."

"If they fail, the mission fails and no one in this room will be around to accept full responsibility," the Ghost said calmly. "Every one of you will be dead or in custody."

"Every one of you?" Rasheed's eyes were wide and his face full of concern.

"What do you mean?" Hakim said.

"He said 'every one of you', not every one of us!" Rasheed continued. "You're not including yourself, sir. What may I ask are your plans?"

The Ghost smiled. "Oh, don't take it the wrong way, Mr. Rasheed. You're being too sensitive. I won't let this mission fail. If the plan is to kill the President and the Prime Minister I can assure you that it will happen. Your plan seems fine, but if it fails, I have a back up."

Hakim paused, looked around the table and then continued, "A back up! What kind of back up?"

"I don't discuss contingencies."

Hakim was unwilling to accept this response.

"Look sir, we don't know you. You were sent here by our leader to aid out cause but your lack of candidness is cause for more concern than comfort," Hakim continued. "We aren't even privy to your name."

"No one is." the Ghost interjected.

"Well, that may be good for you, but it does not satisfy me, or my friends," he gestured to the other men gathered around the table.

There was another long, cold moment of silence and then the Ghost responded.

"Well, what would you have me do?"

The silence continued and he went on. "Do you think that I'm about to change my way of doing things simply to satisfy you people? I've lived this long and been as successful as I am because I work a certain way. Now, you may not like my mode of operation and to be honest with you, I don't give a damn! But Mister Abdula, don't make the mistake of thinking that you and your merry band of men can take me out because I can assure you that won't happen. Trust me when I tell you I'm more than one step ahead of you. I've thought around corners you haven't seen yet."

The group of conspirators stared at the Ghost.

"I think I understand what you're going to do and I know what it is you want of me." He got up, grabbed his coat and walked to the door. "Look, I'm getting bad vibes from this little soiree so I'm going to take my leave."

Suddenly, Hakim exploded and he jumped from his chair. "Sit down, sir. We are not finished."

The Ghost stopped and turned back to Hakim. The expression on his face was one not seen before by any of the people in that room.

"You like life sir?" he asked. There was a deadly coldness in his voice.

"What, so now you're going to kill me?" Hakim said, still fluster in his voice.

The Ghost paused as if thinking about the option. Then he smiled. "No, I'm not going to kill you. I'm going to finish my job.

I'm going to fulfill my assignment. I'm not going to kill anyone, now." He turned and walked out of the room.

The room was silent for at least thirty seconds.

"What the hell was that?" asked Rasheed.

Hakim took a deep breath and looked around the room at his coconspirators. "That was a talking dead man."

"You can't kill him. He's too connected. He was sent here by our leader."

"Our leader has made a mistake. This 'Ghost' person is not one of us. He is a hired gun. I don't know why he was sent to us. We can do this without him." There was anger and resentment in Hakim's voice.

Khan leaned forward on the table. "You kill him and our leader will kill you. No, I take that back. Actually he'll kill all of us."

Hakim looked to his friend. "Khan, he will not be murdered. He will die during our action; when he's done his job and outlived his usefulness. He will die a hero during the mission."

Khan smiled. "Ah, yes, an accident."

"No, my friend, a casualty." Hakim corrected.

Mirad cleared his throat and sighed, "Hakim, what do you know about this man?"

"Not very much," Hakim conceded.

"Well, I have heard of this Ghost person and what I've heard is terrifying."

Hakim stared at Mirad who continued.

"I've heard it said that he's the devil on earth. I didn't know that he was involved in this mission until I was told by you but when you mentioned his name, I knew of him immediately."

"What have you heard?" Khan asked.

"I've heard that he's a master at what he does."

"And that is what?" Ranoud asked.

"Murder, death, terror," Mirad answered. "In my opinion he is the worse kind of terrorist."

"What do you mean, 'the worse kind'? You're speaking nonsense, Mirad." Hakim said.

"I mean, he has no cause, no mission, no great plan. He is a killer who likes to kill, a terrorist who loves to inflict terror."

The room was silent again. Mirad went on.

"And from what I've been told, he is the best in the business."

He leaned toward Hakim. "You say that you're going to take him out. Who is going to do that? This man sees when he's asleep and hears when there is no sound. He can kill you with a shoe string; rip your heart out with a pen knife. I ask you again, Hakim, who will kill this man?"

"I will," Ranoud answered.

Again there was silence as the men absorbed his response.

"I don't know what the leader was thinking or why he is here but I know it must be for a good reason. That being said, nothing will happen until our mission is complete. But when we're through, he will be too."

"You're confident that you can do this?" Rasheed asked.

Ranoud smiled. "My friends, for those of you who do not know of my background, I can assure you that he will not be my first kill."

"I hadn't planned on discussing this but now that we are, let me say that Ranoud is the read master of this type of work. Not only that, he can be trusted. I would bet my life on my good friend and I have many times in the past."

Rasheed shook his head. "We're losing focus, my friends. We came here to discuss our plan, but instead this 'Ghost' person consumes us."

Hakim nodded in agreement. "Rasheed is right. We'll take care of this stranger in due time and in our own way. In the meantime, we must concentrate on our primary mission, to strike at the giant, and rip out its heart. Agreed?"

Hakim looked around the table. All of his guests were smiling.

Chapter Ten

"What do you think?" Caputo asked.

Jack Kane was too engrossed in the remains of the torched car to hear his friend's question.

"Jack, are you with us?" Caputo continued, this time he was a little louder.

Kane stood back from the car and looked up at Caputo. "I think this is the car we're looking for. Look inside." He pointed to the devastated remnants of the vehicle. "There's nothing left behind. I mean nothing. Usually you'd find some trace, a melted pen under the seat, some coins with fingerprints on them in an ashtray, a partial; something, anything. But this burned out baby is squeaky clean. Tom, this is their car." He looked around the scene. "What's the name of this town again?"

"Canonsburg," Tom answered.

"Canonsburg! The name sounds familiar," Kane replied.

"Home of Perry Como and Bobby Vinton," Caputo offered. "Of course they were both before my time."

"I was a big fan of both," Kane admitted. "It was a time when you could understand the music. Today you have a bunch of assholes with their baseball caps on backwards shaking their asses and trying to sound like they're from the ghetto. Most are stupid kids from the suburbs. It's a damn shame if you ask me."

Tom smiled. "Sounds like I touched a sore spot!"

Jack looked back at the skeleton of the SUV. "I know I sound like an old fart, Tom, but I don't know where the hell our society is going these days. Don't get me wrong. I like rock and roll, you know, the Beatles, the Stones, the Eagles, the Doobie Brothers.... but what the hell is with this Eminem? He's a foul mouthed, little prick who needs to get his ass kicked, if you ask me. Little bastard probably couldn't fight his way out of a paper bag."

"I don't know, Jack, his stuff does have a little edge to it. A lot of kids like what he's doing," Tom countered.

"To each his own, I guess." Jack paused. "But I still think he's an obnoxious little prick."

Caputo laughed. "That's why I love you, Jack. There's no holding back."

Kane walked around the car to Caputo. "There's nothing here Tom. Even the VIN numbers have been removed or destroyed. This mess is clean, spotless." He looked intently at his friend. "And that's why I'm sure this is his car. It's been sanitized by a pro. The guy who went through this car knew what he was doing. He knew that we'd be crawling all over this. But there is one thing."

Kane pointed to a section of the car's fender that revealed some of the vehicle's color. "The car was silver. Do you still have the still photo from the cruiser video?"

"Yeah." Caputo answered as he reached into his coat pocket, retrieved it and handed the picture to Kane.

"You know, I really like some of the things about the twenty-first century."

"What do you mean?" asked Caputo.

"Well, back in the old days when I was making a living at this job, pictures like this would have been blurry and black and white. But today, look at that sucker! It's crisp, clear and colorful." Kane smiled. "And, just as I thought, the car our Ghost friend was driving was the exact same color as this one here. The two cars were both silver Honda CRVs. How far are we from the town where this picture was taken?"

Caputo considered the question. "Let's see, no more than five or six miles."

Kane scratched his eyebrow as he took a moment to think something through. "We're going to need some help here. What we've got to do is find someone who saw our fingerless friend in this car. I know it's a long shot, but we're going to have to ask the local departments to show this picture around in convenience stores, gas stations and restaurants in the area. And we're going to need a full court press on this one. They can't start tomorrow, or in a day or two. That could be too late!"

"You want to go to the media?" Caputo asked.

"No. That would be showing our hand. This guy is a pro. He watches everything. Nothing gets by him," Kane answered. "I know this is your jurisdiction and I'm just a consultant here. Ultimately the decision is yours, Tom. As your consultant, however, I would keep our information as close to the vest as possible. If he senses we're on to him, that we're moving in his direction, he'll adjust and alter his plan, and then we're screwed."

Tom nodded in agreement. "You're right Jack. No press, no media. I'll have this picture circulated to every department in the South Hills. I'll mark it 'urgent'. But we can't get our hopes up. It's still a long shot."

"Yeah, I know." said Kane. "But we can't do this by ourselves. If we don't get a break, all we'll be doing is cleaning up after his messes." He pointed to the burned out shell of the car.

"What if we don't get a lead?" Caputo asked.

"We've got to get a lead. I'm afraid something really big is about to go down here, Tom, something terrifying."

"Do you think we should call in the big boys?"

"What, you mean Washington? Sandy's FBI, they already know what's going on here and they're no further along then we are. If we had a battalion of FBI agents working this case they'd only get in the way." Kane paused and then continued. "But don't tell Sandy I said that."

"We're not in a very enviable place here Jack," Caputo offered. "We're both pretty certain something major is about to happen and we're kind of on our own. Sort of sucks doesn't it?"

"Sort of," Kane agreed.

"What do we do while we're waiting for this break?" Caputo asked.

"Well, if they're serious about their canvassing, we should hear something relatively soon. But in the meantime, I have a friend who's pretty high up in the CIA. I want to talk to him."

"I can have a plane fly you down this afternoon. Do you want me to come with you?"

Kane shook his head. "No, you'll have to stay here and hope that we get some positive feedback from the canvass."

"And what shall I tell Sandy?"

"Tell her I had to fly back to New York on some personal business and that I'll be back in the morning. If you tell her that I went to Washington, she might feel that I went around her."

"Which is exactly what you're doing," Caputo added.

"Yeah, well this friend of mine is CIA and you know how territorial these organizations are. If I walk into Langley with an FBI agent I won't get the time of day. If I go in alone... as a retired old friend, I might get everything that I want."

Caputo knew that what Kane was saying was true. "Yeah, and they said that after 9-11 the lines of communication would open up and the departments would be sharing information freely! What a joke. Nothing's really changed, nothing but the rhetoric."

"How do you change fifty years of tradition?" Kane replied. "I think they mean well, but they're huge behemoths who have been doing things a certain way for years. It'll take more than one 9-11 to change them."

Again Kane paused. "Let's just hope we're not on the verge of a second."

The plane ride to DC was uneventful, and Kane liked it that way. He had flown many times in his life, but he never got used to it. Seeing the airliners fly into the World Trade center didn't help to bolster his confidence in the aviation industry either. Oh, he knew about the security methods that had been implemented since the attacks, but he had an imaginative, creative mind and for every new precaution, he had thought of a workaround. Many times he wished that he was just an average traveler, someone who didn't know what was happening behind the scenes. But he wasn't. He was a man who had spent his whole life trying to outsmart the bad guys. He knew that if they wanted to strike again, they could. He also knew that if they wanted to use aircraft as weapons again, they'd figure out a way. These opponents were the worst kind, too. They were people who weren't afraid to die. To them, nothing was sacred except their one fanaticism. They had no problem killing the young or the old, women or children, or all of the aforementioned. Their objective was the complete and total destruction of America. Their mission would not be finished until that objective was fulfilled. God how Kane hated these people. They were a cancer on civilized society and like any cancer there was no guarantee of a cure. And now, as he sat in the back of a cab on his way to Langley, he worried that his beloved country was about to be assaulted again. He felt an awesome and personal responsibility to prevent this attack, but he questioned his ability to do so. Was he in over his head here? Did he have the skills and physical stamina to stop whatever it was that was about to take place?

He was middle-aged and out of shape. Parts of his body ached at times from years of abuse. Arthroscopic knee surgery had removed his left meniscus and slowed him to a fast walk. This getting old stuff wasn't much fun. What was he up against? The last time he had seen the Ghost, it was obvious to Kane that the killer was younger and strong. And judging from the cruiser video he still appeared to be fit and in shape.

Getting to Langley took less time than getting into Langley, but that was to be expected. These were, after all, different and dangerous times. He wasn't unexpected. He had called ahead and asked for the meeting. His friend, Jason Galego, who was the Assistant Director of Homeland Intelligence, had notified security of his arrival. But even an introduction by a high level officer like Galego didn't change the agency's entrance protocol. By the time Kane was in the building, his background had been checked, and checked again. His body had been scanned and his clothing sniffed. He was cleaner than the day he was born.

"God help anyone who had something sharp on them," Kane thought as he walked down the corridor toward the elevators. The elevator was crowded, but there was little, if any, small talk. When the doors opened, an agency official was there to greet him. It was a young woman.

"Mr. Kane, I'm Amanda Cook. I'm one of Mr. Galego's assistants." She was friendly, but all business. She extended her hand.

"Yes, nice to meet you," Kane replied as he shook her hand. He noticed that it seemed unusually cold. Maybe you really did have to be cold and calculated to work in this place!

"Please follow me. I'll take you to his office."

Kane was impressed by the size of the building and all its activity.

"Boy, it's a big, busy place!" he offered.

"Yes, well it is the CIA." There was a supercilious tone in her voice.

"Yes, it is, isn't it?" Kane answered back. "Our tax money at work."

Amanda didn't respond directly to this last remark. Instead she began to prod.

"So, Mr. Kane, what brings you to Langley?"

"What business was it of hers?" he thought.

"A taxi from Reagan."

The woman didn't crack the slightest smile. Obviously she found no humor in his remark.

"Actually I'm one of Jason's old friends." He said trying to sound serious.

"Oh really! Where do you know him from?"

Persistent little devil, he thought.

"We worked on some cases together, several years back."

"You were with the company."

The 'company' meaning the CIA.

"The company! Oh, no. I'm afraid that my career has never been that exciting. I was a New York City detective."

"You're being modest, Mr. Kane. I heard that your career was very exciting." What the hell did this stranger know about his career? How the hell did she know about his career?

"Do we have far to go?" he asked, hoping to put an end to this third degree.

"No, it's just down the hall. So you're working a case?" she went on.

"What? You mean now? No, I'm retired." He tried to fluff off her question.

"Oh really." From the tone in her voice, he knew that she wasn't buying it.

"Actually I'm doing some consulting, just to keep active."

"Consulting! That sounds exciting." She didn't really mean it.

"You can't imagine." he answered, just as they reached an office door with Galego's name on it.

Ms. Cook pulled the door open and held it for Kane. "Well I hope you enjoy your visit to Langley, Mr. Kane. Mr. Galego is waiting for you just inside."

He stepped into the office, the door closed behind him and Ms. Cook was gone. In her stead was Galego's secretary, seated like a sentry in front of two impressive looking wooden doors.

"You must be Mr. Kane." There really was no guessing. She knew who he was. "Mr. Galego is expecting you."

"And you are?" Kane asked.

"Jill. I'm Mr. Galego's executive assistant."

"He has a lot of those, doesn't he?"

"I beg your pardon!" She really didn't make the connection.

Kane gestured to the door. "Ready when you are."

Jill smiled, walked from behind her desk and pushed open Galego's office door.

"Jason, Mr. Kane is here to see you."

Kane entered the room and Jill pulled the door closed as she returned to her desk.

"Jack, good to see you." Galego said as he walked around his desk and shook his friend's hand. "How long has it been? Three or four years?"

"Try seven, Jason," Kane corrected. "This promotion seems to fit you well. I don't think the director had as many assistants, in the old days, as you have now! Nice secretary you've got there."

"You mean Jill? She's no secretary. She's a fully trained agent, with a law degree. She's smart as hell. When she says that she's my assistant, she's exactly that."

"You mean she doesn't type your letters!"

"We all have our own word processors in this place. If you can't type, we have sophisticated dictation software. This is a very hi-tech place, Jack."

"Boy, isn't that the truth. This place has been on the cutting edge of technology since its inception."

"And Jack, these computers do more than take dictation. They do everything but dice tomatoes. They keep you smart," said Galego.

"And they record every word spoken in this room, no matter if it's dictation or not." Kane added. "It's Big Brother in a desktop!"

"How do you know about that?" Galego seemed surprised.

Kane smiled. "You forget, Jason, they were talking about this technology when I left. And speaking of talking, what's with the third degree by Miss Cook? Did someone blow my cover? Does she know that I once worked here?"

Galego shrugged his shoulders. "What makes you ask that, Jack?"

"She met me at the elevator and pumped me like an old inner tube until I got to your office."

"Look around you Jack. You're in the headquarters building of the damned Central Intelligence Agency. Everyone here is trained to asked questions and to never accept an answer at face value. Besides, she works for Jack Sorenson and he's a competitive, nosey bastard. He probably saw your name on the daily Intel register and did some checking. I mean there are other people in the firm who know that we placed you in the NYPD. It's not like your name isn't known around this place, Jack."

"Yeah, but I thought my cover was top secret. Remember, the CIA wasn't supposed to be doing that kind of stuff; not in the good old US of A. I don't think people in the hallways should be talking about me or my work, do you?"

Galego, although only in his early forties, was a twenty-year veteran with the CIA. He had leading man looks and the intelligence of a Brown University honors graduate, which was appropriate because he was a Brown University honors graduate. He had all of the qualities that one would need to climb the corporate or, in this case, agency ladder. Early in his career, he had, on occasion, worked in the field with Kane. But that was the old days. Now he was upper level CIA management. Now Galego was only a few promotions from the pinnacle of espionage power.

"No, they shouldn't," Galego agreed. "But again, this is the Central Intelligence Agency and our business is getting answers to questions. Now, don't worry about that. Sit down and tell me why you're here."

Kane walked over to a high backed side chair and did as instructed.

"Jay, what is the latest on our friend the Ghost?"

Galego's eyes widened. "Why do you ask about him? Are you going after your old nemesis in your retirement?"

"You might say that," Kane said, carefully weighing his response.

Galego walked to his chair and sat down. "You know Jack, you don't work here anymore. We're not supposed to give out our Intel to every Tom, Dick and Harry who walks in off the street."

Kane smiled. "Jay, I'm not just some Tom, Dick or Harry. I'm your old buddy and I need a favor."

Galego paused again and then turned to the computer on his desk.

"I don't know, Jack. I shouldn't be doing this," he said as he typed a few commands on the computer's keyboard.

"Hey Jay, it wouldn't be the first time that we stretched the rules." Kane smiled.

Galego leaned in toward the computer screen and read the information. "Wow! It would appear that our old fingerless friend has been busy. And take a look at this!"

Galego turned the flat screen monitor toward Kane.

"Recognize the guy he's with?" Galego asked.

"It looks like that bearded asshole from Saudi Arabia!"

"If it's not him then there's some other tall goofy looking guy walking around out there, who looks just like him," Galego continued.

Kane was still staring at the picture. "When was this taken?"

"About five weeks ago, by the Israelis.

"Do you know where it was taken?"

Galego turned the screen back to him and punched in a few more keyboard commands. He waited for a moment and then looked up at Kane.

"It says here, Tehran."

Kane leaned back in his chair. "Well that would make sense. Last I heard Iran had become the country of choice for discriminating terrorists. Do you have any idea why these two were meeting?"

"Nothing concrete, mind you, but we think something very big is about to come down and we're pretty sure they've hired our friend here to help things along."

"How big is 'pretty big'?"

Galego sighed a little and said, "Something that will make 9-11 look small."

The two men were silent for a moment.

"Jack, what's up? Why are you asking about the Ghost?"

Kane looked down at the floor for a second, as if mustering the strength to tell his old friend the truth.

He looked back at Galego. "He's here, Jay."

"Who's here? The Ghost?"

"That's right. He's involved in something up in Pittsburgh."

"Does it have to do with that airplane explosion?"

"Yes, I think so." Kane answered. "But I'm getting the feeling that the attack on that airplane was only the tip of the iceberg. Furthermore, I think that that was only the beginning, a diversionary action."

Then Kane went on to tell Galego all that he knew, which he realized wasn't very much when he was finished.

"The FBI's in on this right?" Galego asked.

"Yes, but I don't think they realize the scope of this thing, just yet."

"Jack, with this new Department of Homeland Security setup, I can't jump into this thing. The FBI's running point on this."

"Yeah, I know," said Kane.

Galego thought for a moment and then went on. "But this doesn't mean that I can't help you. I'd love nothing more than to bring this bastard down. The FBI's not going to let me get involved directly, but what they don't know won't hurt them. If things go well and they get the credit, that's fine with me. It means that there'll be one less bad guy out there trying to kill my people and that I like."

"What have you got up your sleeve?" Kane asked.

"Nothing terribly complicated." Galego was thinking and talking at the same time. "I'll start gathering all the Intel I can find on Mutt and Jeff here and you keep me informed as to what the hell's going on up there in Pittsburgh. I'm not asking you to spy on the FBI or anyone else working the case. I'd rather you think of me and the agency as a personal resource. You'll call my direct line and speak to me and only me. I don't want anyone in this building to know what's going on. If it gets too big for the two of us, we'll cross that bridge when we get to it."

"And you can get me more info than the FBI?" Kane asked.

"Jack, come on, you worked here. What do you think?" asked Galego. "Besides, the FBI thinks that you're a retired old New York City cop."

"Which I am."

"Yeah, but they don't know of your CIA connection. Even if they have the same information that I have, they're not going to share it all with you. You know that."

"I know." Kane agreed.

"It sounds like you're on to something here and it's big."

Kane leaned toward Galego's desk. "Jay, I need to know if you've been following any suspected terrorist cells in the Pittsburgh area. To be more specific, the southern suburbs of Pittsburgh."

Galego's eyes widened. This time he didn't need to refer to the computer. He knew the answer.

"Actually, Jack, we've been keeping an eye on a small group of middle eastern immigrants who, we suspect, are a terrorist cell."

"Suspect?" asked Kane.

The handsome intelligence officer hesitated for a moment and then continued.

"All right, Jack, maybe we more than suspect that they're a terrorist cell."

Kane was taken back a bit by his answer.

"Wait, you people know that these guys are terrorists and you haven't taken them down! What about that explosion at Pittsburgh International Airport? Didn't you guys make the connection?"

"Of course we did," Galego said sounding a bit perturbed.

"Some people were killed in that explosion," Kane continued.

"Yeah, well we think that most of them were working for that cell."

"How about those that weren't working for the cell, the ones who were just poor slobs working in the wrong place?" Kane asked, raising his voice a little.

"Hey Jack, the CIA isn't perfect. We do our best, but sometimes that just isn't good enough." Galego said as he angrily tossed a piece of paper into the waste basket next to his desk.

"Jay, what would have happened if that bomb didn't go off prematurely and that plane made it into the air with two hundred people on board?"

Galego thought for a moment, sighed and said nothing.

Kane leaned back in his chair. "It would have been a hell of a mess, Jay. It could have been another 9-11."

"We know that Jack. We spend twenty-four hours a day, seven days a week in this place trying to make sure that that doesn't happen again."

"But it almost did."

Galego looked across the desk straight into Kane's eyes and said coldly, "Sometimes you have to let little things happen in order to stop the big things."

"Oh, for crying out loud Jay, that's nonsense. You mean that the CIA knew that something was going to happen at that airport and you didn't do a damned thing?"

"Jack, sometimes you can't tip your hand early or you'll lose the game."

Kane sat in silence for a few seconds.

"I don't know how you do it, Jay."

"What do you mean?"

"How do you people get to a point where you can rationalize tragedies?"

Galego was slow to respond. "It's not easy Jack, it's not easy."

"So, there is something big going down in Pittsburgh?" It was more of a question than a statement.

"I can't tell you much, Jack. This is an ongoing investigation, and it's classified."

"All right then, but you do acknowledge the existence of a terrorist group working out of Pittsburgh?"

"I told you that much already."

"You mind if I ask how you know?"

Galego raised his eyebrows but didn't answer. It was answer enough for Kane.

"Oh!" The word was long and drawn out. "You have someone on the inside."

Again Galego was silent but the look on his face said, "Yes."

"Good. Well then at least give me the name of the guy running the cell. We think the Ghost is working with him. Right now, we're spinning our wheels. All we're doing is cleaning up his messes."

"You screw up this case Jack and I'll have you thrown into a federal prison." Galego said as he punched a few keys on the keyboard.

"That might be an interesting place to spend my retirement," Kane said smiling.

"You'd probably like it." Galego was still looking at the computer screen.

"Okay, we're looking at a guy named Hakim Abdula. He and his wife, Dana, arrived in this country about eight years ago. Shortly after they got here, they opened what was to become a very successful, multi-million dollar trucking company."

"You can't be looking at them just because they built a successful business," Kane said.

"It's not that they simply built a successful business, Jack. It's that several times along the way they were on the verge of bankruptcy and from out of nowhere they were flush again. They were getting large infusions of cash to keep that trucking company alive."

"Do you know where the cash came from?"

"We think we do. Their business is trucking. They have eighteen wheelers rolling all over the United States and Canada, too. We think the money was coming in from the north, carried across the border and over the road to their headquarters by those very same trucks."

Kane rubbed his eyes. The lack of sleep was catching up with him. "These weren't just hard working people who were lucky enough to rescue themselves from disaster each time?"

"No." Galego said definitively. "We looked into these people. Their business wasn't all that good. Their rates were too high and their service wasn't anything to speak of. They didn't have a big clientele. And at each and every point of collapse, nothing would change business wise that could justify their sudden turnarounds."

"How large were these infusions?"

"A couple of million dollars each time."

"Were they ever audited?"

"Three times. And each time they buried the money and made it all look legit."

Kane looked impressed. "Wow. It's not easy to justify chunks of money like that."

"No, it's not." Galego agreed. "But I can assure you Jack that they were taught how to do that, long before they got here. Al-Qaeda isn't all guns and masks. Hell, their leader's a billionaire. They know how to move money around."

"A trucking company," Kane went on, "Amazing! What a perfect business for a group like this. It gives them a network and a way to move material and equipment around the country. How'd you find out about them?"

Galego got up from behind his desk. "Jack, you know I can't tell you that. Hell, I've told you too much as it is."

"And you have someone working the inside?"

Again Galego didn't answer.

Kane smiled. "Well Jay, at least you're consistent."

"That's my middle name. I hope I've been of some help," he said in a way that suggested that their tête-à-tête was over.

Kane got up from his seat and straightened his coat jacket. "I think you've been a big help. At least we have a direction, some place to look."

Galego took a deep breath. "Well, there is one caveat."

Kane knew what was coming. "There always is in this place."

"Our investigation is ongoing. You know what that means, Jack. It's active. We've got people working this thing. This is a very delicate situation that we're both in. Obviously you people have to work the case, too. But you can't screw it up for us, Jack. The only reason why I told you what I told you was because I didn't want you to stumble into this situation with guns drawn and bullets flying. Now there's a good chance that your friends would never have found this cell. But the problem is, you're in on the investigation and you have a very uncanny way of uncovering the uncoverable."

"I'll take that as a compliment," Kane grinned.

"Yes, well take it anyway you'd like, but you have to promise me that you'll keep me in the loop."

Kane said nothing.

Galego went on. "Jack, you've got to promise. This is a national security situation. We need your help, too. If it looks like your people are going to crash the party, you've got to let us know. If you don't, some good people might be hurt."

"I'll do my best," Kane answered. "I realize that you're talking about your guy inside."

Galego was still standing behind his desk. "Guy inside! I never mentioned a guy inside. But it might affect innocent bystanders. You disrupt this nest and these assholes just might pull the pin. You know what I mean, in the name of Allah."

"I'll do what I can, Jay, but I'm not running this investigation. I'm just a 'consultant'." Kane reached across the desk and shook Galego's hand.

"Well then do some creative consulting. It's important," Galego said, as he returned the handshake.

The two men started to walk toward the door.

"I wish there was time to have dinner with you, but I've got meetings for the rest of the afternoon."

Kane knew that this wasn't the truth but he was anxious to leave, too. "No problem. I've got to catch a flight back to Pittsburgh. They'll be wondering where the heck I am."

They reached the door and Galego pulled it open.

"Remember, keep me in the loop."

He evaded that instruction again. "Good seeing you again. Thanks for your time."

And with that Kane turned and left the office. Galego stood in his office doorway and watched his old friend walk to the elevators. The elevator doors opened, Kane turned back to Galego, waved 'good-bye' and disappeared into the car. Once the doors closed, Galego turned back to Jill and said, "Get me the Director, now."

Chapter Eleven

Tom Caputo was late arriving at the airport and when he drove his car into the arrivals area, in front of the Landside Terminal, he could see Jack Kane waiting patiently on the sidewalk. He pulled over, rolled down the passenger side window and yelled to his friend.

"Didn't I first meet you this way?"

Kane smiled, hurried to the car and got in.

"Have you been waiting long?" Caputo asked.

"Not really. Maybe ten minutes."

Caputo could see that there was something on Kane's mind.

"What's up?"

"What do you mean?"

Caputo gestured to his friend's face. "You look like you're carrying the weight of the world on your shoulders. Did you get bad news in Washington?"

Kane loosened his tie and opened the top button of his dress shirt.

"The CIA's full of bad news. They're in the 'bad news' business." Kane continued, "But, I got the information that I was hoping to get."

Caputo steered the car away from the terminal and started for the airport exit.

"Well, are you going to keep me in suspense all the way back into Pittsburgh? What did you find out?"

"I found out that there is an active terrorist cell working in this city."

"You did!" Caputo sounded surprised. "Did you find out where?"

"In the southern suburbs."

"The South Hills," Caputo corrected.

"Yeah, right, the South Hills."

"What else did you find out?"

"I found out that they've been on the CIA's radar screen for some time."

"Why haven't they closed them down?" Caputo asked as he glanced up at his rearview mirror and noticed a set of headlights swing into position right behind his car.

"Because they want to use them to get to the big guys, the people at the top."

Caputo looked back at the road ahead. "Do they really think that a cell in Pittsburgh is going to lead them to the leaders of Al-Qaeda? It sounds to me like a long shot."

Kane was staring out into the darkness. "You see, Tom, here's how it works with our friends at Langley. They treat every possibility as if it's their only possibility and they attack it with everything they've got. The CIA may be pursuing ten other long shots, just like this one. And believe me, they have the money and the resources to go full throttle on every lead, and they do. So it may be a long shot, but we've got to be careful. Big Brother will be watching us too."

Caputo glanced at the mirror again. The same car was keeping pace. "You know, that may explain the set of headlights behind us."

Kane turned around and looked back at the car. "What? You think that's a tail?"

"I've tailed and I've been tailed. He's not very subtle about it, but I think they're following us. He dropped in behind us when we hit the expressway and he's kept pace ever since. He's had plenty of opportunities to pass, but he hasn't."

"Well, we haven't been on the road very long. It could just be a coincidence. Maybe he's just one of the guys who like to tailgate."

"Yeah, maybe," Caputo said, sounding unconvinced.

Suddenly Caputo swung the steering wheel hard to the right and the car swerved sharply and quickly on to an exit ramp.

"Wow!" was all Kane could say.

Caputo looked at his mirror in time to see the tail perform the same maneuver; only the split second difference caused him to smash through some abutment barrels as he struggled to make the exit.

"Is he still there?" Kane asked.

"He may need some body work, but 'yes' he's still there."

"Well then that answers that question. My friend at Langley has his boys tailing me."

"With friends like that…" Caputo left it unfinished.

They crossed the small road at the bottom of the exit and took the access road back to the highway. The tail followed right along.

"It has to be CIA. Who else knew that you went to Washington or what time you'd be returning?"

"This is standard operating procedure. From now on, they'll be one step behind us."

"Great! Maybe you shouldn't have gone to Washington."

"Hindsight is twenty-twenty," said Kane. "Actually, they probably knew about us right after the plane blew up. They knew someone had to be investigating the case. I'm sure the fact that the FBI was on the scene wouldn't have stopped them. As a matter of fact, in this case they might be working with the FBI."

He paused, as if considering that possibility, and then continued, "But I think the information that we got was worth it. Don't worry about them. Assume that they'll hear and see everything, and work the case as you'd normally work it."

"You don't think they'll step in at the last minute and screw it up?"

"They may step in, but they won't screw it up."

"How do you know?"

"Because we won't let them."

Twenty minutes later they were parked in front of the Pittsburgh Hilton, at Gateway Center. The tail rolled to a stop a half a block away.

"You like staying here?" asked Caputo.

Kane smiled. "I have some fond memories of this place."

"Yeah, like the night you threw that guy, who was trying to kill you, out of your window."

"That was a night I'll never forget."

Caputo adjusted his rearview mirror to get a better look at the car that was following them. "It looks like a typical government-issue black SUV."

"You'd think that they'd be a little creative with their choice of cars and color schemes," Kane said.

"So what's next? Where do you think we should go from here?" asked Caputo.

Kane rubbed his eyes and sighed. "I'm not sure. This is a very complicated situation. We've got a murder case and an act of terror to investigate; we've got an active terrorist cell operating in our backyard; we've got a cold blooded psychopath who calls himself the Ghost and we've got the FBI and CIA running their own separate investigations and watching our every move. Everywhere we turn there's an obstacle. It's like trying to walk through a minefield, on an elephant. I think we should sleep on it and get a fresh start in the morning."

Caputo liked the idea. "I agree. I'm beat, too. I just hope that things are clearer in the morning."

"I do, too." Kane said as he pulled the door handle and opened the door. "Thanks for the ride Tom. I'll see you at your office in the morning."

Kane stepped out of the car, put on his overcoat and started to walk toward the SUV. Caputo knew what he was doing immediately and adjusted his rearview mirror to get a better view. Kane wasn't hurrying. It was a slow, casual walk. He stopped at the driver's side and tapped on the window. After a moment of hesitation, the window opened slowly. The driver seemed unsure. He said nothing and didn't turn fully toward Kane.

"Look guys, I don't know why Galego gave you this assignment, but I'll do what I can to help you out. I'm going in now. I'm going right to my room; I'm going to the bathroom, because I always get constipated when I travel, then I'm going to take a shower, maybe have a snack and a soda and then I'm going to hit the sack. Oh, but the first thing I'll do when I enter my room is give it a good sweep. You never know what kinds of bugs you'll find in even the best hotels these days and if I find any I'm going to flush those expensive, high-tech toys down the toilet where all that crap belongs. Now, if I were you, I'd call Langley and tell them that this 'tail' thing is a waste of time. I mean after all there's got to be something more productive for you to do, right? Good night guys."

Kane turned, smiled at Caputo as he walked by his car and walked into the hotel. He entered the lobby and looked back at the SUV. It was still there. He knew it would be. He would have gotten the same result talking to the water fountain in the front courtyard. These were trained government-issue human androids. They were issued instructions and nothing would or could prevent them from doing their duty.

Kane walked through the lobby to the main bank of elevators and pressed the call button. He looked at the status lights above the doors. All of the cars were near the top of the building and headed in the wrong direction.

"Just my luck," he mumbled. "I'll spend the rest of the night waiting for the damn elevator."

For the first time since he accepted this assignment, he felt depleted, like a drained battery. While he waited, he began to ask himself why he took this case. He didn't need the work. He hadn't taken it for the money. He had all the money he needed. The book rights to the Johnny Reece case had made him a rich man. Reece was a major league pitcher who moonlighted as an assassin for a Pittsburgh crime family. Kane had traveled to Pittsburgh, the first time, to find out who killed an old informant friend. By the time he left the city, he had solved the case and made a new friend in Tom Caputo. The book, entitled Squeeze Play, had become a bestseller and made him a national celebrity; a position that made him, more often then not, uncomfortable. But there was so much more to Kane than money and fame. He was addicted to the entire investigative process. The more complicated the case, the better he liked it. He loved the challenge of solving the unsolvable. He liked doing what so many others couldn't do.

"I must really be a sick puppy." he thought as he waited.

The ring of an arrival bell, followed by the doors opening on the elevator directly in front of him, interrupted his daydreaming. The car's only occupant was a man, dressed in an overcoat with the collar pulled up and wearing a baseball cap, with the brim pulled down to partially cover his eyes. Kane waited a moment for the man to exit. Their eyes met briefly as he stepped past the detective. When they did, something registered. Kane stepped into the car and looked back at the stranger. He was only able to catch a fleeting glimpse of the man who disappeared around a corner and was gone.

"Get a grip," he said to himself. "Not everyone's a bad guy."

But he couldn't shake the feeling that this stranger was no stranger. The elevator ride was short and his room was just a few doors down. Suddenly he realized that he was standing in front of his door. Funny, he hardly remembered getting there. He was still thinking about the man wearing the baseball cap.

"Why was it pulled down in the front? Was he trying to hide something?" His mind was racing. "I had to work to see his eyes and when I did, they looked familiar and they were looking right through me!"

Kane fumbled for his card key and then inserted it in the lock. The code was accepted and the lock released. He started to turn the doorknob and was about ready to push the door open when an image flashed in his mind and he stopped. Those eyes… he had seen them before. They were the piercing, cold, deadly eyes of the Ghost.

"Son of a bitch!" Kane said out loud, as if to someone standing right next to him. He pulled the Ruger P85 9mm from the holster under his jacket, jacked a round into the chamber and slowly began to open the door. He stopped and moved his hand along the frame and then the door to see if there were any booby trap wires. It seemed clean. Carefully he opened the door the rest of the way and then, without entering the room, reached in and flipped on the lights. Nothing happened. All seemed normal. He entered cautiously and moved directly into the bathroom. He yanked the shower curtain open, but there was nothing behind it. He checked under the towels, inside the coffee maker, under the bathroom counter and all around the toilet. Everything was the way it was supposed to be. He moved back into the room, did a quick scan and then pulled open the closet door. The only thing it hid was an iron and its board. He reached back and closed the entrance door. It looked as if the last people in the room were from housekeeping. Nothing appeared to be out of place.

Kane activated the safety on his gun and slipped the weapon back into its holster.

"You're getting to be an old lady," Kane thought. "Now you're starting to imagine things."

He took off his coat and threw it on a chair. Then he unfastened his shoulder holster, removed it and placed it carefully on the nightstand next to the bed. He was turning back to the television when he noticed, what appeared to be a small bump in the bed sheets, and a half dollar sized dark red stain.

"What the hell is this?" he asked as he grabbed the sheets and slowly pulled them back.

"My God!" he said as he stared down at the bloody remains of what appeared to be a woman's finger. It was the little finger and it had been removed, just above the knuckle, with a procedure that appeared to have been performed by a butcher and not a surgeon. There was a bloodstained note next to the severed digit. Kane took a pencil from the nightstand drawer and, using the eraser, slowly and meticulously opened the page. It read, "I read where you were in town and I thought I'd stop by and give you the finger. By the way, how is Miss Ryan?"

"Oh no!" Kane said, thinking the worst.

He took Ryan's business card from his shirt pocket and dialed the number. It rang several times before her voice mail answered.

He waited for her greeting to end and then said, "Sandy, this is Jack Kane. Call me on my cell as soon as you get this message. This is very, very important."

Kane left the number and hung up the phone. Then he called Caputo who had just arrived home.

"Tom, get over here as fast as you can. Our friend the Ghost just paid me a visit and he left a woman's finger in my bed. I think it might be Sandy's."

"Sandy's finger! What makes you say that?"

"The son of a bitch left a note and, although he didn't come right out and say it, he implied that it might be hers."

"Did you try calling her?"

"Yeah, and I got her answering machine."

"Not good," said Caputo. "I'll call the office and have the boys run over to her house."

"No, Tom. Don't send a squad car. We should go," Kane said unequivocally.

"All right, I'll meet you out front in fifteen minutes. You know Jack, we could be jumping to conclusions."

"Yeah, well it's someone's. If it's not hers then there's some other poor bastard out there walking around with a bloody stump where a finger used to be."

"If they're walking at all," Caputo added. "Fifteen minutes, out front."

Kane was out front in ten minutes and Caputo was waiting there to meet him. Normally, the ride from the Pittsburgh Hilton to Sandy's condo in Mount Lebanon was a fifteen-minute drive. Caputo made the trip in less than ten. He had lights on and the siren screaming all the way and he raced down the narrow city streets at speeds that approached seventy miles an hour. Kane kept dialing Sandy's phone number, but all he kept getting was the answering machine.

Ryan's condo was half of a two family duplex condominium in a fashionable section of the suburban Pittsburgh community. Caputo had been to her place before so there was no searching for house numbers. He knew where she lived. He swerved the car into her small driveway and the vehicle jerked to a stop.

"I don't see any car," Caputo said.

"That could be a good thing." Kane concluded.

"The place is dark. It looks like no one's home."

"Let's find out," Kane said, his door already halfway open.

The two men hurried to her front door and Kane rang the bell several times. They waited. Nothing.

"What do you think?" Kane asked.

"Try it again." Caputo answered, pointing to the doorbell.

Kane rang it again, this time longer and more deliberately. Again they waited. Suddenly, a light came on inside and they heard movement. The deadbolt released, the chain was unfastened and the door was pulled open.

"Hey guys! What's up?" a sleepy Sandy Ryan asked.

"What's up?" Caputo sounded relieved and a bit irritated at the same time.

"Well, we're glad to see that you are," Kane answered. "May we come in?"

"Of course," Ryan said, sounding a little embarrassed that she hadn't made the offer first.

Caputo and Kane entered her front room and were quiet for a moment.

"Well boys, you didn't come out to see if I kept a clean house. What's going on?"

Kane had noticed that the house was clean and tastefully decorated. It was a pleasant and warm home, obviously maintained by someone with class.

"You have a lovely place Sandy." Kane offered.

He paused, cleared his throat and continued.

"Sandy, the Ghost broke into my room tonight."

"My God!" her response was almost involuntary.

"He put a woman's severed finger in my bed…"

"With this note." Caputo handed Sandy the bloodstained piece of paper.

Sandy read the message.

"Obviously you thought it was me."

"Yup." Kane said.

"You know, I have stationery just like this," she continued.

"Have you been in all night?" Caputo asked.

"No. I was at the mall doing some shopping. I got home about forty-five minutes ago."

"Why didn't you answer the phone?" Kane asked.

"What are you talking about? I haven't had any calls!"

"The hell you haven't." Kane corrected. "I must've called your answering machine fifty times!"

"I don't have an answering machine. I have an answering service that answers and stores all my messages at the phone company."

"Wait a second, your phone could be down and you'd still be able to take messages?" Caputo asked.

"That's right," she said. "It's one of the advantages of the service. You never miss a call. Even when your phone is out of order, the service continues to take messages."

"How many phones do you have?" asked Kane.

"Just two. One over there," she pointed to a phone on an end table next to a couch, "and one upstairs. They're both portables so I can really use them in any room."

Kane stepped around a coffee table and walked over to the telephone. At first glance everything seemed normal. Then he noticed the telephone jack lying on the floor.

"He was here." Kane sounded angry. "The bastard was here."

"What? He was in this house?" Sandy asked.

"That's right." Kane pointed to the telephone cord. "He disconnected your phone. When you check upstairs you'll probably find that one on the floor, too."

"Everything looked okay when I came home!"

"Yeah, but you said the stationery looked familiar. It's probably yours. He came here tonight looking for you," Caputo offered.

Sandy seemed stunned.

"Why don't you sit down?" Kane suggested.

"I don't know how he could have broken in without my neighbor hearing him." She was trying to put the pieces together. "Flora is a nice person, but she's a bit nosey. I'm surprised she didn't greet you at the door!"

"When you're living alone, sometimes having a curious neighbor can be a good thing." Kane said, in an almost fatherly way.

"Not when you're trying to have a romantic evening with a gentleman friend." Sandy disagreed. "And you know she has a glass to the wall."

That was more information than Kane needed.

"Oh, ah, yeah, I guess so," he fumbled. "I see what you mean."

"Can I see you stationery?" Caputo asked.

"It's right over here." Sandy walked a few steps to a small roll top desk, opened a side drawer, and retrieved a small box of paper. She took off the cover and gasped.

"Well if there was any question about him being here, it's been answered." She tilted the box toward Kane and Caputo. On the top sheet were written two words: 'ANOTHER TIME'.

"I think we should have a talk with your next door neighbor," Kane said.

"I agree," Caputo added.

"Follow me," Sandy said, pulling the belt a bit tighter on her bathrobe and walking out the front door, Kane and Caputo in tow.

Sandy knocked on the neighbor's door and to her surprise the door moved.

"It's open!" she said. "Flora!"

She pushed the door the rest of the way and yelled again. "Flora! It's Sandy next door!" Still silence.

"Something's wrong here," she said. "Killer should have been all over us by now."

"Killer!" Caputo didn't like the sound of it. "What the hell is a 'Killer'?"

She smiled. "Relax, Tom. He's a lovable little mutt about the size of your shoe. Look at him crossways and he runs in the closet."

"Sort of like how I used to react to my ex-wife," Kane added. Both Sandy and Caputo laughed.

The domicile was dark. The only light on was a small night light in the hallway.

"There's got to be a light switch around here somewhere," Caputo said as he ran his hand along the wall.

"Over here," Sandy said as she flipped a switch and a single overhead light went on. "I don't get it. She never leaves the house. She's always here."

"Always?" Kane asked, sounding unconvinced.

"Always," Sandy said emphatically. "She even has her groceries delivered. I don't think I've ever seen her go past her mailbox."

Kane led the trio as they continued on to the kitchen, which was in the back section of the house. Everything was in place. The table was clean, there were no dishes in the sink and nothing was left out on the counter.

"Well she's not a messy housekeeper," Caputo commented.

"You've got to do something to pass the time, if you're in the house all day," Kane said. "I think we'd better check the upstairs."

The three detectives did an about face, walked back down the hallway to the staircase and started up. As soon as Kane reached the top step, he noticed a familiar smell. The three detectives stopped.

"You smellin' what I'm smellin'?" Kane asked.

"I'm afraid so," Sandy answered.

"Nothing's as distinctive as the smell of warm blood," Caputo continued.

"Oh damn," Sandy said softly.

Kane noticed that there was a light on in the room at the far end of the hallway.

He reached for his 9mm. "Better safe than sorry."

"I hope she's not just reading in bed, with earphones on. She'll have a friggin' heart attack," Sandy said in a lower, whispering voice.

"Actually, I hope she's reading in bed," Caputo said.

Kane resumed the search, walking slowly toward the end room. The closer they got, the more pungent the smell.

"It smells like a damned slaughterhouse," said Caputo.

Kane paused at the doorway and then stepped into the room.

"Well, there's your reason why," he said.

Flora was lying on the bed; eyes wide open and locked in death. Her body was contorted and her nightclothes were drenched in blood.

Sandy looked and then turned away, "Dear mother of God."

Kane walked around the bed and discovered Killer. The little dog was on the floor, twisted and dead.

"The bastard even broke the dog's neck."

"Jack, over here." There was urgency in Caputo's voice. Kane returned to the other side of the bed.

"She's missing a finger." Caputo pointed to her hand, which was dangling over the side of the mattress.

Sandy was trying to understand what was going on. "You mean he couldn't find me so he came over here and killed Flora?"

"That's the way it looks," Kane answered.

"But why? What's his reasoning behind this?"

"He's doing this to taunt me."

"Oh this is unbelievable. He's murdering strangers to get your attention!"

"The prick must really hate you," Caputo said.

"I don't know much about the guy except for the fact that I had a run in with him once; he shot me and I shot him."

"Well you really got his attention," Caputo continued.

"I wish you were a better shot." There was coldness in Sandy's voice.

"Yeah, I wish I was, too," Kane agreed.

"I'd better call downtown and get a crew over here.

Sandy turned to Jack. "This monster is fearless, Jack. He broke into your room, my house and then Flora's. Did you see any sign of forced entry?" she asked. "I didn't."

"No, neither did I," Caputo agreed.

Kane holstered his weapon. "You wouldn't with this guy. He's not an amateur. This might appear to be an amateurish vendetta, but it's not. It's his way of getting his kicks."

"Is this your stationery, too?" Caputo asked as he pulled a paper from Flora's mirror. "Do you believe this guy?"

He turned the note to his companions. It read: WELL I HAD TO FIND A FINGER SOMEWHERE!

"Next time you shoot him Jack," Sandy said. "Shoot him in the nuts?"

Chapter Twelve

The Ghost was already in the warehouse when Ranoud entered the building and switched on the lights. The mercenary was sitting in a chair at the far end of the room, a single overhead light illuminating his presence. His voice startled Ranoud.

"And I thought you people were always prompt!"

Ranoud froze.

"Do you always make it a practice to break into buildings?" he asked.

"Who's breaking in?" the Ghost said defensively. "Why, I thought we were all on the same team here. Don't I have as much right to be here as you, Mr. Safad? If I remember correctly, this building, no this business was financed by the man who sent me here; and you here, too."

The Ghost got out of his chair. "You may have a key, Mr. Safad, but I have as much right to be in this building as you, maybe more."

Ranoud walked to his desk and placed his coat over the back of the chair.

"If that's the case, and you're one of us, then why refer to us as 'you people'?"

Ranoud heard the Ghost laugh. "Well, let's not kid each other. I'll be the first to admit that there are differences, significant differences. For example, you fight for your religion. I fight for myself. You believe that your world will be a better world. I believe that this is as good as it will ever get. But we can't let these differences get in the way of the success of our mission, can we?"

Ranoud was becoming impatient with the intruder. "Do I have to stand here and listen to your bullshit? Hell, you won't even tell us your real name! You drop into our lives, uninvited mind you, and all of a sudden our world is turned upside down! Our plans have to be adjusted to fit your needs because, after all, our leader sent you to us. I'll tell you Mister whatever the hell your name is; most of us have begun to question our leader's sanity. What was he thinking when he hired you? We have been working on this mission for the better part of six years. We've had to be patient and flexible. We've built a team of trusted soldiers, some of whom are ready to sacrifice their lives for the sake of this undertaking. And let there be no doubt about it, some of them will die on the day of this attack. No, this is not about our religious or philosophical differences. Personally, I don't care if you pray to Allah or howl at the moon. I'm upset, no; we're upset because you have become a distraction. You intimidate some of my friends, but you don't intimidate me. You piss me off." Ranoud stopped and took a deep breath. He was angry now and if he didn't reign in that anger it could be boiling over and God knows what could happen then. "But that's counter productive. My being pissed off doesn't help the mission. It's one of those distractions I was telling you about."

The Ghost smiled. "Well Mr. Safad, you're much more passionate about your work than I had thought! I'm sorry if I appear to be a distraction. It was not my intention. I remain anonymous because I don't want to get caught. There are people all over the world who have dedicated their lives to capture and or kill me. I've found that the use of the 'Ghost' moniker has its advantages. To my knowledge, even the most sophisticated intelligence gathering organizations in the world have little if anything of substance on the real me. They've done a lot of guessing, but they've got nothing. Now, if you think that I'm going to change my mode of operation just to satisfy you then you are sadly mistaken. You're pissed off? So what! Do you think I care, Mr. Safad? Not in your wildest dreams. I don't care if I'm not on your Christmas card list. Oh, wait… maybe that's the wrong holiday."

Ranoud thought for a moment. His pistol was just inside the top desk drawer. He could casually open it, as if he was getting some keys, and he could have the gun in his hand in a matter of seconds. He could eliminate this Ghost character in mere minutes. One quick round to the center of his forehead and this wise guy would be out of their lives. He could hear the sound of the gun and see the flash from the muzzle, the round spinning toward its target, the penetration and blood splatter of the wound, the emptiness in his eyes, the collapse of his legs and the fall to the floor. He could see all this. Then reality set in. Everyone Ranoud respected said that this killer was always a step ahead. Would he let his guard down? Could he be so careless? He thought again. He could see the desk drawer open and then the gun in his hand. He could feel his finger squeeze the trigger and then hear the sound of the hammer click on an empty chamber. He could see the man smile as he reached into his coat pocket and withdrew a silenced pistol. The barrel appeared to grow as the mercenary raised the weapon to fire. Ranoud felt frozen, locked in place and unable to move. He imagined the muzzle flash and then heard the explosion of the round. It seemed odd that the flash came before the sound, he thought. Now he could see the bullet spinning in his direction. This daydream moved in slow motion, he could see almost every revolution. He couldn't move! The fear was overpowering.

"Do they have Ramadan cards?"

Suddenly, everything he imagined was gone, the bullet, the gun, his impending doom.

"What?" Ranoud had lost his place in the conversation.

"Ah, another surprise!" said the Ghost. "First I thought that you were punctual and now I see that you have a hard time staying focused! I'm starting to wonder if you possess the skills needed to be a part of this endeavor."

The Ghost reached across the desk and handed Ranoud a handkerchief.

"You're sweating." he said as he gestured toward Ranoud's forehead.

Was he that nervous? Was he that upset? Ranoud paused and dabbed the cloth against his face.

"I'm fine." Ranoud said defensively. "I'm just not feeling well."

"Is it the mission that's upsetting you?"

"Hell no. I'm fine with the mission."

"Maybe it's too much for you. Maybe you should step aside," the Ghost continued.

"My life is this mission. My sole purpose for being is to help make this happen."

"That's pretty dramatic. You must really hate these people."

Ranoud placed the handkerchief on his desk and glared across the desk at the Ghost.

"Hate? Yes I hate them and everything that they stand for. This society is a cancer on our world. They have no morals, no deep religious values. They embrace pornography and homosexuality. Why they defend and promote it. They allow their children to dress like thugs and to listen to and chant vile street slang. They let their women meddle in the affairs of men. They're overfed, overindulgent vermin and like all vermin they must be destroyed."

The Ghost smiled. "Well, I guess I've touched a nerve."

Ranoud said nothing, preferring to pause to gather his thoughts.

"You've done some thinking about this, haven't you?" asked the Ghost.

"What do you really want? Why are you here?" Ranoud was calm now.

The smile faded as the Ghost began his response. "I wanted to know a little bit more about one of the key players in this exercise. I wanted to learn more about you."

"And have you learned something?"

The Ghost walked a couple of steps closer to Ranoud. "I think that I have! This hatred of yours... it really is a part of you, isn't it? Some people wear their hatred, but you're different. It's not on your face; it's in your soul. It's almost as if you were born with this anger."

"I never took you for a psychoanalyst," Ranoud replied.

"You see, that's where I'm consistent, Mr. Safad."

"Consistent?"

"Yes, I'm consistently unpredictable. You never know what I'm going to do or say next."

"Let me ask you a question, Mr...Mr. Ghost. Are you fully prepared for this attack?"

"Prepared? How do you mean?" The Ghost wanted clarification.

"I mean, how much do you know about what's going to happen?"

The Ghost smiled again. "I know everything."

Ranoud shook his head. "Not even I know everything about this mission."

"Well, then I guess I know more than you."

"I don't believe you. How could you know more than me? I helped plan this mission."

The Ghost had a smug look on his face. "I know that Friday evening, during the height of rush hour, tanker trucks filled with fuel will explode on all the major tunnels, roads and bridges leading into Pittsburgh. I know that the explosions will be synchronized and they'll trigger when the President of the United States and the Prime Minister of Israel are both inside the convention center. I know that emergency communications systems will be overwhelmed with distress calls. I know that snipers will be stationed at strategic locations in the city to randomly pick off responding police and emergency vehicles. I know that the key to the success of this operation is panic, confusion and general public chaos. I know that the vials that I brought to the Abdula's home are absolutely worthless."

Ranoud interrupted. "What do you mean worthless?"

"I mean that your plan was changed."

"What are you talking about? How could it have been changed without us knowing about it?"

"I'm telling you now. The concentrate would never have worked. It dissipates too quickly."

"But I thought…"

The Ghost continued. "It becomes harmless in a matter of seconds. The only people who would die would be the people handling the stuff."

Ranoud was trying to piece it all together. "But you led us to believe that the concentrate was a useful weapon!"

"No… you already were convinced of that. I just allowed you to continue thinking that way."

"But why? For what purpose?"

The Ghost became very serious. "Because I didn't know you people. I couldn't trust you."

"What makes you think that you can trust us now?"

"Well, for one thing you didn't try to go for your gun in the desk drawer."

Ranoud looked down at the desk and then back to the Ghost.

"Of course it would have been a mistake if you had," the Ghost said as he dropped a handful of bullets on Ranoud's desk.

Ranoud leaned back in his chair. It wasn't making any sense to the man. "But Hakim told me that you showed them the concentrate at their house when you arrived!"

"I showed them two metal cylinders."

"Vials," Ranoud corrected.

"Vials, cylinders, whatever. All they saw were two empty metal containers."

"Empty! Wasn't that a bit risky of you, bringing empty containers to their house?"

The Ghost grabbed his chair and dragged it closer to the desk. "I knew they wouldn't open it. They couldn't open it. They were convinced that the containers were filled with one of the world's deadliest toxins. They believed that the smallest amount of this poison could kill thousands of people."

Ranoud was having a hard time processing all of this new information. "But I don't understand. Why the duplicity? Aren't we all supposed to be on the same team? Isn't that what you just said a little while ago?"

The Ghost slowly sat in the chair, as if he were considering his answer. "Look, we are all supposed to be on the same team. But, to be honest with you Mr. Safad, we have learned that some of us have a different agenda. We can't tell the entire team about the change in our plans because not all of them can be trusted."

Ranoud looked puzzled. "But surely you can trust Hakim and his wife."

It was more of a question than a statement.

The Ghost did not respond. He simply stared quietly across the desk.

"You can't trust them?" Ranoud sounded very surprised.

The Ghost sidestepped the question.

"Let me say that we think that we can trust you. And that's why I'm here."

"Of course you can trust me. There is nothing in my life more important than our cause and this action." Ranoud said emphatically.

"Good. That's what we wanted to hear," the Ghost answered, smiling somewhat insincerely. "Now would you like to know what really was in the cylinders?"

"Yes I would."

The Ghost leaned forward in his chair. "We were never really convinced that this plan would work the way Hakim had envisioned it. Bio chemicals and poisons are too unpredictable. They really don't have much of a track record."

"We always knew that there would be a risk." Ranoud admitted.

"Risks are fine when you're playing a game or some sport. But with something this important, you can't afford risk. You mustn't accept the possibility of failure. You must expect, no, you must demand success. That being said, it was decided some time ago to change key elements of this mission." The Ghost stood again and began to pace in front of Ranoud's desk. "We decided to replace the poison with one of our portable nuclear devices."

"A suitcase nuke," Ranoud said.

"Yes," the Ghost stopped and turned to Ranoud. "They have been called that."

Ranoud's eyes were wide. "I had heard that we might have these things, but I never really believed those stories. I mean, who has nuclear weapons?"

"We do," the Ghost answered.

Ranoud sat quietly for a moment and then continued, "How much damage can one of these bombs do?"

The Ghost smiled and considered the question. "Well, they really haven't been tested yet. These aren't exactly the same nukes that disappeared from the Soviet Union after its collapse. Don't get me wrong; we did buy most of those. It's just that our experts weren't satisfied with their design. They were created in the eighties and there's been a lot of technical development since then. Our guys wanted a bigger bang for our buck."

"A bigger bang?"

"We figured that if we're going to make the effort to explode a nuclear bomb, it's not going to be some silly little thing that takes out a few blocks. If we're going to plant a bomb in the middle of a city, it's going to destroy the entire city."

"I thought that our target was the President and the Prime Minister!"

"They are, but our fight is not simply with them. It is with this whole country and everyone in it."

Ranoud thought about the response and then continued, "Wait a second. You said 'our fight'. You've already admitted that you're not one of us. You're a mercenary, a soldier for hire."

"Good point. But you have to understand, Mr. Safad, that a professional soldier, or a mercenary as you put it, has to be totally committed to the side that is paying him." He smiled a broad, toothy smile. "You're earning interest with God and I'm earning interest with my bank. Our compensation may be different, but our goals are the same. You want to kill America for your own religious interests and I want to kill America for my own financial interest. The fact is we both want to kill America."

"You still didn't answer my question," Ranoud continued. "How much damage will this bomb do?"

"If we place it in the convention center and detonate it when the President speaks, it will incinerate him instantly and vaporize everything within a one mile radius, in less than a second. Pittsburgh will be history. We estimate that as many as a hundred thousand people will die."

"A hundred thousand," the figure rolled slowly out of Ranoud's mouth.

"Of course they'll be all over the city, but the convention center alone will be filled to capacity with an audience of about twenty thousand," the Ghost said matter-of-factly. "Hell, they won't know what hit them."

"None of this seems to bother you," Ranoud observed.

"Should it?"

"It's one thing to kill the President and the Jew, but a hundred thousand people!"

"Ah, you surprise me again, Mr. Safad. You're a terrorist with a conscience." The Ghost moved a step closer to Ranoud. "Look, our job is to destroy this nation. It's a big job. Some may say an impossible job, but I think it's very doable if done properly."

Ranoud said nothing and just listened.

"In order to bring this Giant down, you must take it out at the knees. You don't take it down with a tap. You have to destroy its legs." The Ghost's eyes were wide and his delivery intense. For the first time, Ranoud could hear insanity in the Ghost's voice. "There is a feeling around this globe that the United States of America is invincible. I don't share that opinion. I think that, in the whole world, there isn't a weaker, more vulnerable country. It is top-heavy with success and excess. It is like a spoiled small child. It has had too much, too fast. In less than three hundred years this land of nothing has become rich, fat and arrogant. It thinks of itself as a policeman, I think of it as a bully. It claims to be the land of the free and the home of the brave. Yeah, well it's really the land of the decadent and the home of the corrupt, if you ask me. Why, this country won't know what to do with itself after we attack it."

"But nine-eleven…"

The Ghost finished Ranoud's sentence. "…was nothing. It was a training exercise compared to what we have planned. Think about it Mr. Safad. With the press of one button we will eliminate the President of the United States, the Prime Minister of Israel and a hundred thousand of our hated enemy. What more could you ask for?"

Ranoud thought for a moment. He was here to kill the President and Prime Minister. America was his enemy. It's just that the thought of killing a hundred thousand people was a bit much to comprehend.

He took a deep breath. "It's an amazing change of plans. We're not going to simply kill the President and Prime Minister. We're going to kill a city."

"An American city," the Ghost clarified. "And when we kill this city, we're going to take out America's legs. It will begin to fall and when a giant with no legs falls, it can't get up. Once it's down, it's so much easier to kill."

Ranoud stood, turned, walked a few steps from his desk and then turned back to the Ghost. "Why are you here talking to me? Why is it so important that I know this? Hakim has been our leader. Shouldn't he be told? I've known him for years. He's passionate about our cause. No matter what you have heard, he can be trusted."

The Ghost thought for a moment and then answered. "Our leader, your leader, feels that we can trust you more."

"So where does this leave Hakim and his wife?"

"They're not to be told about the change in our plan."

"You're not going to tell them?"

"No," the Ghost said absolutely. "As far as they are concerned, the cylinder contains a bio-toxin. As far as they're concerned, we're making only one significant change and that is that they, personally, will be given the honor of triggering the device."

Ranoud thought for a moment. "But wait. They think that their protective measures will keep them safe. They believe that they'll be able to escape. The original plan calls for a delay between triggering time and detonation of the weapon. It sounds as if this new plan has no escape and they'll be killed with everyone else."

"Martyrs for the cause," the Ghost said coldly.

The two men were quiet again.

"Do you really have a problem with that?" the Ghost asked. "You said that the movement meant everything to you, didn't you?"

"Yes," Ranoud replied.

"Well, we can tap the giant or we can knock him down and kill him. What would you rather do?"

"Knock him down and kill him, of course. It's just that... Hakim and his wife dying weren't in the plan."

"Mr.Safad, every time a giant falls it lands on something, right? Unfortunately, this time, when this giant falls, it will land on Hakim and his wife," the Ghost smiled and continued. "Ah, but the good news is, the giant will fall."

"Hakim has been a loyal member of our organization. He's never done a thing to warrant this action."

The Ghost became very serious. "Well, look, Mr.Safad, someone has got to trigger the bomb. If not the Abdulas, then it will have to be some other senior member of this cell. Maybe you wouldn't mind setting it off!"

Ranoud did not hesitate to answer. "No sir, that's not for me. I'm not a suicide bomber. Ask me to do any number of things, but don't ask me to kill myself because, I'll tell you right now, that is one thing that I could never bring myself to do."

"I didn't think so."

"Why does it have to be a senior member of our organization?"

"You don't want to entrust this responsibility to someone from the rank and file. It must be handled by a person with a sincere commitment."

"But why? They don't know it's a suicide mission. If they think that they're going to get away, anybody can do it."

"You want this handled by someone who understands the importance of doing this right. You can't have a private doing a general's job. Our soldiers will block the bridges and blow up the trucks, but the Abdulas, this group's leaders, will pull the pin."

"And die," Ranoud added.

"Many will die," the Ghost finished.

Ranoud thought for a moment.

"They won't do it," he said matter-of-factly. "Hakim is not stupid. He didn't get to where he is in this organization by making stupid choices. I'm sure he'd think that pulling the pin was a dumb move."

"Then he'll have to be ordered to do it. It will be your job to help reinforce the command. If he hesitates or has second thoughts, you'll have to give him a nudge. If it's obvious he's going to back out then I'm afraid you'll have to kill him."

"Me! Why me?"

"Because he trusts you."

"You're telling me that not only do I have to convince my friend that he should stand next to a nuclear bomb and then trigger it, but if he doesn't do that, then I've got to kill him? This is crazy!"

"Mr. Safad, you're either committed to this mission or you're not. Are you committed?"

"If I say that I don't want to help kill my friend then that means I'm not committed?" Ranoud asked.

"You're looking at this the wrong way. You have to focus on the results."

Ranoud shook his head. "Why can't this be remotely detonated?"

"How? With a cell phone? The Secret Service will be jamming all cell signals within a five-block radius of the convention center. Maybe you were thinking of a timer? They've proven to be unreliable. Sometimes the President is late to arrive at a function by as much as two hours. How do you set the detonation time? If you want to guarantee that the President and the Prime Minister are taken out in this attack, then the person who sets it off has to be in the building and see them with his own eyes. That's the only way to be sure of its success."

Ranoud stood quietly, considering what the Ghost had said.

"This is the movement's biggest effort. It will make 9-11 look like a small skirmish. You're not destroying a couple of buildings, you're killing a city. This will be the twenty-first century's Hiroshima, only bigger. This will be America's mortal wound."

"If you're so passionate about this, then why don't you set it off?" Ranoud said softly.

"Me? No, that's not my job, Mr. Safad. Remember, I'm not a full fledged member of your organization. I'm a hired gun."

"But you seem to be passionate about this mission."

The Ghost grinned. "I'm passionate about every job that I take. Granted I hate America, so that makes this job a little easier, but I'm not really one of you. You have your faith, and it's a faith that I don't embrace. Don't take that the wrong way, Mr.Safad. I don't embrace any religion. As I've said before, I believe in one thing - me."

"What makes you hate America?"

"Years of living in this cesspool, with my eyes open. It's a vile, despicable society and I can't wait for it to implode," his voice seemed full of anger.

"An American who hates America!"

"Who said I was an American?" he snapped back.

There was a moment of dangerous silence.

"Enough about me," the Ghost said in a way that signaled that this part of the conversation was over.

Ranoud could sense a shift in the mood of the conversation. The Ghost had been calm, persuasive and convincing. Suddenly, he sounded angry and threatening.

"Okay, if it can be done, I'll do it."

The Ghost considered the answer and then smiled again. "Good. Trust me Mr. Safad, it can be done."

"You do realize that this is a big sacrifice for me," Ranoud added.

"Not as big a sacrifice as Hakim and his wife will make."

The Ghost seemed to enjoy toying with Ranoud's emotions.

"He may not listen to me. He may insist that a subordinate do it."

"Then you have to convince him of the importance of obeying orders that come from your leader. I'd suggest that you do that in front of the entire group. He wouldn't think of challenging an order from the Big Guy, in front of them. They'd turn on him in a heartbeat, if he were to do that." The Ghost's demeanor changed and it was apparent to Ranoud that this meeting was coming to an end. "Mr. Safad, I guarantee you that he'll be next to that bomb when it goes off. Remember, he'll think that he's simply arming the device and that he'll be able to slip away. He'll also understand that if he doesn't follow these orders he'll loose the respect of his people and everyone else in the organization. Hakim thrives on respect. Why hell, it's part of your culture. And of course, last but not least, he'll also realize that he'll be killed."

The Ghost turned and walked half way to the door and then turned back quickly to Ranoud.

"So we're on the same page here, Mr. Safad?"

Ranoud was now standing behind his desk, looking somewhat defeated.

"Yes… yes we are," he replied, sounding a bit dejected.

The Ghost grinned again. "Good. I knew you'd be reasonable." He did a one-eighty again and quickly left the building.

Ranoud stood quietly for a moment, trying to absorb what he had just experienced. Slowly, he sat back in his chair. He paused again and then took out his cell phone and carefully dialed a number. A moment later, someone answered at the other end.

"Hakim, my brother, we have a problem." He then went on to explain the entire confrontation and conversation that he had just had with the Ghost. Not a fact was left out. When he was finished, they were both silent, considering their options.

"Okay, this was not unexpected," Hakim said to his friend. "We knew that we couldn't trust this stranger. How he wormed his way into our operation is beyond me. That being said Ranoud; two can play this duplicitous game. I'm actually glad we're using a suitcase nuke. But I can assure you, Ranoud, neither I nor my wife will be standing next to that thing when it detonates."

Then something else occurred to Hakim. "You're not on a regular phone are you?"

Ranoud was now leaning back in his chair. The day had just begun and he was already exhausted. "No, Hakim. I'm not that naïve. I'm using my cell phone."

"Good. Let me think about how we're going to handle this. It's obvious that something else is going on here, at a different level. We have to be careful."

"Should you contact our leader?" Ranoud asked.

"No. We don't know who we can trust back there. We have to handle this here.

We will eliminate this problem ourselves and then tell anyone who asks that he was a casualty of war. They'll never be able to blame us if it appears that he was killed by the opposition."

"You're right. That's the way it should be handled."

"Relax, Ranoud. We'll take care of this," Hakim reassured his friend. "This Ghost character will be a real ghost soon."

A few moments later their conversation was over. Ranoud flipped the cell phone closed and shoved it back into his pocket. He took a deep breath and appeared to look relieved.

The Ghost turned off the small receiver that monitored the eavesdropping device he had planted in the warehouse.

"Okay, so here we go," he said out loud to himself.

He turned the ignition, pulled the car into gear and drove away.

Chapter Thirteen

Kane waited for Galego to come to the phone. In the old days, when the detective was active, the wait would have been short. But things had changed. As far as Galego was concerned, the older agent was no longer a first string player. His call was considered more interruptive than informative. Kane wanted to hang up, to tell the younger man to "go screw himself," but he knew that it was all part of the game. He'd just have to be patient and wait.

The deafening period of silence was broken when Galego answered at the other end. "What's up Jack? You got more news on our Ghost friend?"

"Jason… can you stop the President from coming into Pittsburgh today?"

"Hell no, Jack. He's committed." Galego was emphatic. "He's already on the road. It's a three city stop and Pittsburgh is the end of the line."

"I'm afraid that it may be the end of the line in more ways than one," said Kane.

"Jack, I don't know what you've got, but they've had Secret Service in that town for nearly a month preparing for this trip."

"And the plane explosion at Pittsburgh International wasn't enough to make them change their plans?"

"Hey, this president doesn't back away from terrorism. You know that Jack. Besides, it's an election year. How do you think it would look if he were to cancel this trip now? The Prime Minister of Israel is going to be there. That man lives with terrorism every day of his life. The President's opponents would be all over this like flies on crap. I could see the headline now: Prime Minister of Israel Stood Up in Pittsburgh by Anxious President-Rumor of Terrorist Attack Sends President Scurrying Back To Washington. Hell, he might as well book the moving van right now because, sure as shit, he'd be out of the White House in November."

Kane knew Galego was right. "That's assuming he lives to November."

"Get to the point, Jack. What's going on? What do you know?"

"I know that this Ghost character isn't in town on a vacation. I think that his bumping into me was an accident and that he's here to do something far more sinister than to kill me." Kane ran a hand across his unshaven beard. "I need more from you, Jason. I know that you have more and I need it."

Galego was quiet for a couple of seconds. "I don't know Jack. I could get into a lot of trouble…"

"And if something happens to the President you could get into a lot more trouble," Kane finished.

Galego didn't say anything so Kane continued. "Jason, you said the other day that I would have direct access to you, that I could think of you as a resource. I was supposed to be able to call you directly and you'd be right there. Well hell, pal, I called your direct number and got your assistant! Not terribly direct is it? She put me on hold for over ten minutes! I thought you wanted this open line of communication between us? Jason, I can't help but think that you're bullshitting me."

"I'm sorry if you've come to that conclusion Jack." Galego said somberly.

"Hey, I'm sitting in a rented car, in front of my hotel building, unshaven and very tired. That being said, this is just the beginning of my day, Jason. And the way things look right now, I've got a feeling it's going to be a tough day." Kane paused, rubbed his eyes and then went on. "Tell me more about this Hakim."

"Like what?"

"Like who's your plant on the inside?"

"I can't tell you that! I've already told you too much," Galego snapped back.

"Hey, we're not playing a game here kid. This is not some territorial thing. There's a good chance something is going to happen to the President of the United States in this town, and we've got to stop it."

"You're new to this investigation, Jack, and I think you're jumping to a lot of conclusions."

"Nonsense. We've got an active terror cell working out of the suburbs and there was the attack at the airport. A known, world class killer is in town and two major world leaders, who you have to know are right there on the very top of the Al Qaeda hit list, are speaking here in front of the friggin' National Conference of Christians and Jews. You call that jumping to conclusions? Come on Jason, it doesn't take a rocket scientist to figure this one out."

"All right Jack, but you've got to promise to keep anything I give you close to the vest."

"Hey, it's all going to be a moot point by this time next week. Besides, you already told me about Hakim and his lovely bride."

"Our man is a guy who goes by the name of Mohammed Khan."

"How do I get a hold of this Mohammed Khan?"

There was a long pause in the conversation.

"Jason? It's not a hard question. No multiple choice here," Kane said angrily.

"Well, to be honest with you, I don't know."

Suddenly the tired detective was wide-awake. "I don't like the sound of this. What do you mean you don't know?"

"The last time we heard from him he was headed for a meeting in West Virginia. That was yesterday."

"Nothing since that meeting?"

"No. It's like he fell off the planet."

"What were you able to get from him before you lost contact?"

"Not much. I know he was working them slowly."

"Slowly?"

"Yeah. It takes a while to win these people's trust. We know that they're planning a major assault. He was supposed to get the specifics in West Virginia. Oh, and in his last contact he mentioned a new member who had just arrived from Europe, a guy who was missing a finger."

Kane knew who it was. "The Ghost. Any pictures?"

"No. We were hoping to get those after his West Virginia meeting. Obviously something happened in West Virginia that forced him to cut off communication."

Kane leaned against the steering wheel. "How often was he supposed to check in?"

"Twice a day, morning and evening."

"And what was your contingency plan if he didn't?"

"If I don't hear from him by noon, I'm to do everything in my power to stop the President from visiting Pittsburgh. Look. This is a tough situation. Maybe he has a good reason for not checking in. We just can't go pounding on his door. That might blow his cover, or even worse, get him killed."

"Can you trust him?"

"Who?"

"Can you trust this Mohammed person?" Kane said more deliberately.

"Absolutely. He's a well trained agent, he's one of us, and his real name is Joe Silvia. He's from Fall River, Massachusetts and he's as American as apple pie. The guy's a Harvard graduate with a major in Middle Eastern languages and culture. He minored in drama and he's an amazing actor. Silvia can make you believe that he grew up in Yemen and that he's the only son of a poor shop owner. He speaks the language better than most natives." Galego continued, "Jack, we just got him into the cell. It took some pretty fancy footwork to pull it off, too. He hasn't been with them two weeks."

"What were you people going to do if he didn't check in; just pretend he never existed?" Kane sounded miffed. "This is not good, Jason. Agents don't miss their contact times unless there's a problem."

There was silence.

"Okay, where does this guy live?" Kane went on.

"Jack, you can't blow his cover."

"I have no intention of blowing his cover. I'll be very discreet."

Kane could hear Galego shuffle some papers. "Let's see. He's living in a townhouse that we own in a town called South Fayette. The address is number four, Quail Hill Run. Do you know where it is?"

"Come on, Jason. You're talking to a guy from New York. I'm lucky if I can find my damned hotel. But, I'll find it. How hard could it be?"

"Four, Quail Hill Run, South Fayette?" Galego repeated.

"I got it the first time," Kane said as he started his car. Just then the passenger door opened and Sandy Ryan got in.

"Ah, look, I'll check it out and get back to you," he said, weighing his words in front of Sandy. "I've got to go. Stay near the phone. I'll be calling you again soon."

Kane closed the cell phone and tossed it into the center console.

"Well this is an unexpected surprise. I thought you'd be getting used to your new digs!" said Kane.

The attractive young woman smiled. "Can you believe this asshole killed my neighbor? It just doesn't make any sense."

"You can't expect him to 'make sense'. The guy's a mean prick."

"If it were up to me, I'd still be in my apartment."

"Hey, staying in a hotel for a couple of days won't kill you. As a matter of fact, staying home might! We really don't know what this lunatic's thinking. Yes, it might be directed at me, but then again he may have another agenda. We can't afford to take that risk. I'm glad you made the move. Where are you staying?"

"Right there." She pointed to the Pittsburgh Hilton.

"I guess we're neighbors!"

"I guess."

"Well, I've got a few things to do and…."

"I'm going with you." Sandy said definitely.

"Wait, I…"

Sandy interrupted him again. "You're running a lead. I can see it in your face and I heard it in your voice, when you were on the phone. I want in, Jack. I need to be in."

Kane didn't like the intrusion. "Look Sandy, I'm not sure exactly what I'm doing here. Yes, I'm looking into something but it's probably a waste of time."

"Well then, let's waste some time together. Besides, I can't hang around the office and twiddle my thumbs, and I sure as hell can't hang around a hotel room."

"I don't know," he said, as he tried to make up his mind.

"Besides Jack, you're a civilian and I'm an FBI agent. I can get more doors open with my badge than you can with your beautiful Irish smile."

"If only she knew," Kane thought, thinking of his CIA connection. He pulled the car into gear and accelerated on to Fort Duquesne Boulevard.

"I guess this means that I can come!" Sandy said as she secured her seatbelt.

Pittsburgh is a unique city. What makes this big thriving metropolis different is that you can be in the wilderness of Western Pennsylvania within minutes of leaving the downtown area, traffic permitting. Drive across the Fort Pitt Bridge and then out through the tunnel of the same name and you're in the wooded suburbs. Head east for five minutes and south for ten and suddenly you're in an area where there are probably more deer than people. In New York City it's not uncommon to find cars stripped and abandoned alongside the highway. In Western Pennsylvania it's dead deer carcasses that litter the roadways.

"Boy, there must never be a shortage of venison out here," Kane commented as he passed his fifth or sixth deer corpse.

"I've never had it," Sandy said, with a touch of disdain in her voice.

"You live in hunter heaven and you've never had deer meat?"

"No. I'm one of those kids who cried at Bambi. I could easily shoot the Ghost but I find the idea of putting a bullet in a poor innocent deer abhorrent."

"I can understand that. One is a monster and the other's a defenseless animal."

They drove along in silence for a while and unexpectedly Kane found himself thinking about where he was and why he was there. This was crazy, he thought. He should be home, enjoying his retirement. But here he was, racing around the Pennsylvania countryside looking for a world-class killer and his murderous cohorts. But why? The FBI was on the case. The state police had it covered. And even his old employer, the CIA, was working the case, albeit in a somewhat clandestine fashion. But he knew that he had to be doing what he was doing. It was the right thing, he thought. There were so many reasons why he should be there; the airplane attack, the presence of the Ghost, his insatiable appetite to search for the truth and, of course, his unabashed patriotism all contributed to his involvement.

"This is the exit," Sandy said, interrupting his daydream.

He had almost passed it. Kane braked abruptly and turned hard to the right, just in time to make the exit.

"Boy, you are from New York, aren't you?" said Sandy.

"Hey, I made it," Kane said defensively.

"But you left my stomach back on the highway."

Kane smiled. "I drive this way all the time. I never had an accident in my life, or a ticket for that matter."

"All that means is that you're a lucky driver and not necessarily a good one."

Kane looked to the right and the left at the end of the exit ramp.

"Which way?"

"We go left here," Sandy answered. "The condo complex should be a mile or two down the road."

Kane spun the steering wheel to the left and accelerated through the intersection.

"You act like you've been here before!"

"I used to date a guy who lived out in the area."

"He had to be a farmer."

She grinned, "No, actually he was a millionaire real estate developer whose house was bigger than my old high school."

"How did you let that one slip away?"

"I found out that he swung both ways."

"What? He was bi?"

"Well, let me put it to you this way. When it came to sex, he was very flexible."

Kane was quiet for a moment and then continued, "Well you know what they say about bisexuality."

"What do they say about bisexuality?"

"It doubles your chances of getting a date." Kane laughed.

Sandy simply smiled.

A few minutes passed and they were at the main entrance to Quail Hill Run. It was an attractive and well-maintained middle class condominium community.

"Which one are we looking for?" Sandy asked.

"Number four and it's right there," he answered, pointing to a unit that was two down from the entrance.

"And who are we here to see?"

"Look, I brought you along for the ride but why don't you just sit in the car?" He stopped the car in front of the condo and shut off the motor. Sandy was the first to get out.

"Sit in the car and be a nice little girl! I don't think so," she said sarcastically. "Now, who are we meeting?"

Kane got out and walked around the front of the car to Sandy.

"You're a willful little wench, aren't you?"

She didn't reply.

"Okay, the gentleman's name is Mohammed Khan."

"And why are we here to see Mister Khan?"

"To make sure that he's still alive."

The answer surprised her. "You mean that he might be dead?"

"He might be."

"Boy two dead bodies in less than twenty-four hours. That would be a personal record for me," she said soberly.

They started up the walkway to the front entrance.

"Well, we haven't found anything here yet."

"What makes this Kahn guy so important?"

"He's one of us. He works with the Central Intelligence Agency."

Sandy stopped dead in her tracks. "And how would you know that?"

She already knew too much, Kane thought, but he realized that she was onto him. He could lie, but she would see around it. He turned back to her. "In another life, in another time, I used to be affiliated with the CIA."

"Affiliated?"

"Affiliated." He wouldn't define the word any further.

She took a deep breath. "But you're not anymore?"

"Well, not directly."

"Oh, it's sort of like the mob, once you're in, you're in for good."

Kane raised his eyebrows. "Well I never really looked at it that way before, but I guess you're right."

He stepped a little closer to Sandy. "I used to be a CIA operative."

"And here I thought that you were just a little old city cop; kind of like your ordinary everyday Columbo type."

"I was recruited by Central Intelligence in the mid-seventies. There were a lot of things going on in New York back in those days. The FALN was blowing things up, headquarters had a problem with corruption and there was even talk of foreign agents working amongst New York's finest. I had been in Military Intelligence. They decided that they needed some reliable people on the inside and it didn't take them very long to search me out."

"Wasn't that like spying on your brother officers?"

Kane looked around and realized that they were having this deep conversation in the middle of the condominium's front yard.

"Look, this is neither the time nor place to be having this conversation. Let's continue after we finish what we have to do here."

"All right." she said, nodding in agreement.

The couple turned and continued to the front door.

"What do we do if there's no answer?" Sandy asked.

"We break in," Kane said without hesitation.

"Boy, for a law abiding citizen you're sure fast with an answer that'll get us thrown in jail."

"Relax. I have friends in the FBI."

"Great."

The wait seemed inordinately long but the rattle of the lock and then the door being pulled open broke the silence.

"Hi. Mister Kahn?" Kane asked.

The man hesitated and then answered. "Yes. What can I do for you?"

He had a deep Middle Eastern accent and looked like a person from that part of the world. Then Kane realized that he didn't have a plan for actually finding the man. Now what? He wasn't even certain that the individual standing in front of him was actually the agent or simply someone pretending to be Kahn. He had never even seen a picture of the man.

Sandy picked up the ball that Kane had dropped. "A mutual friend of ours in Washington said that if we were in town that we should look you up."

Kahn took a short breath and then opened the door all the way.

"Please, come in."

The couple accepted the invitation and stepped inside.

Kahn checked to see if there was anyone else, then closed and locked the door. When he turned toward the couple, he had a gun in his hand.

"What is going on?" he demanded, still with the thick accent. Kane was starting to think that maybe he had made a mistake, a deadly mistake.

"No, wait a second pal, there's no need of that," said Kane as he raised his two hands as if to surrender. "Jason sent us."

Kahn paused as if to decipher the information. "Jason! Jason who?" he questioned.

"Jason Galego," Kane said as he slowly lowered his hands.

"And I should know this Jason Galego?"

Kane nodded, 'yes'.

Kahn lowered the handgun, walked a couple of steps to a desk and placed the weapon in a drawer. "Boy, I sure hope you two are legit," he continued with all traces of the accent gone.

"You're Joe Silvia from Massachusetts, right?" Kane said.

Kahn rolled his eyes. "God, I hope that the Boston accent isn't slipping through. I'm a dead man if Hakim hears it."

"Trust me, you're fine." Sandy reassured. "You're incredibly convincing."

Kahn motioned to the living room. "Why don't we go in here and sit down."

The couple followed his lead and moved to chairs in the sparsely decorated room.

"We really can't stay very long," said Kane. "The reason we came by was to make sure you're still alive. When you didn't check in they started to get worried down in Langley."

Kahn nervously scratched the back of his head and then pulled aside a curtain on the front window, as if to see if he was being watched.

"There was no way that I could call in."

"What about your cell?" Sandy asked.

"They took it and replaced it as soon as I was introduced to the others. Thank God it was new and I hadn't used it yet. There were no questionable numbers in its history; just the untraceable numbers the tech guys programmed into it before I got it."

Kane scanned the room. "And you don't have any other phone?"

"I think they've got a tap on everything."

Sandy looked down at the floor and then back to Kahn. "That can't be. Couldn't you have used a payphone somewhere?"

"Everywhere I go, out there," he pointed to the front door, "I swear I'm being followed."

"Are you sure?" Kane asked.

"Look, this group is unbelievable. And they're on top of everything! You should have seen the sweep I did of this place. I pulled this joint apart, not that there's much to pull apart. Fortunately, I didn't find anything. But, for all I know they're listening through the walls."

The more he said the more nervous he became. "These people aren't to be played with. You can tell Jason that they're planning to hit the convention center tomorrow. They want to kill the President and the Prime Minister. They're going to use a bio-toxin, I think."

Kane leaned forward in his chair. "You think?"

"Well, that's what they're talking about at the meetings, but there's a wild card in this game. He calls himself, the Ghost."

"I know who he is."

"He's thrown a monkey wrench into the deal. He's sort of placed himself in charge and… "

"And?"

"And, he's caused some serious concern amongst the ranks."

"You think he's playing straight with them?"

"I don't know! I don't think anyone else in the group does, either."

Kane looked over at Sandy. "What do you think?"

"I think we've got to do something to protect the President."

Kane got out of his chair. "I've got to ask you, Kahn, or Silvia, or whatever the heck your name is, were you ever planning to warn the President or were you just going to hang out here?"

Kahn's face reddened. He stood up and took a step toward Kane. He was angry. "Look mister, I don't know who you are, but I do know how to do my job. My instructions were that if I couldn't reach Jason by noon, he was to contact the White House to try and stop the trip.

"No pal, you don't know me. If it were me, I would have figured out a way to make contact, period."

Kahn didn't say anything. It looked as if he was thinking about taking a swing at Kane.

"I wouldn't if I were you." the older detective said, picking up on Kahn's body language. "I may look like a worn out old guy…"

He gestured toward the door. Sandy took the cue and they both started in that direction.

He turned back to Kahn and finished the sentence, "but I'd kick your ass."

"Get the hell out of here," Kahn yelled. "Before we put it to the test."

The couple made their exit a moment before Kahn slammed the door behind them. He was furious.

"Who the hell are you?" he yelled to an empty room. He walked slowly into the living room and looked out the front window, just in time to see Kane's car drive away.

"You old bastard." He was still talking to himself. "You walk in here like you know me and you pull that crap!"

Kahn went into the kitchen, opened a cabinet door and took out a glass. He grabbed a bottle of scotch from the kitchen counter and quickly poured himself a glass, making sure that he had left enough room for the ice. He got that from the ice dispenser on the refrigerator door. Kahn leaned against the counter, fuming. He stirred the drink with a finger and then downed a generous mouthful of the beverage. Glass in hand he sauntered back toward the living room.

"How dare you come in here and accuse me…" Kahn was still mumbling when he was interrupted by a knock on the front door. He took another quick drink. "Now who the hell is this?"

He moved the front curtain aside. The visitor was standing just out of his view. Again, there was a knock on the door.

"Okay, okay!" he said in a loud voice.

Kahn went to a desk in the hallway, opened a drawer and again took out his 9mm Berretta. He chambered a round and then continued to the door. He hesitated and then leaned forward to look through the peephole.

"Now what?" he said, recognizing the visitor. "Suddenly this place is as busy as Grand Central!"

Kahn put the gun down on the desk, then slid the security chain aside and released the deadbolt.

"Talk, talk, talk, everyone wants to talk," he continued, as he pulled the door open. He was so into his rant that he didn't see the blast from the visitor's silenced Walther. The round caught him squarely in the middle of his forehead and ripped off the top part of his skull. There was no question about the results. Even to the untrained eye, it was easy to see that the Kahn, or rather CIA undercover agent Joe Silvia, was dead.

Chapter Fourteen

Tom Caputo had spent the first part of his day trying to find his two friends. He had called their rooms and then tried their cell phones but the rooms were empty and the cell phones were off. Caputo didn't know where the two of them were or what they were doing but he did know that he didn't like being left behind, on the sidelines. In the short time that the three of them had worked together, he had come to think of their relationship as a Three Musketeers kind of thing. They were an inseparable trio, or so he thought. This morning, however, he felt abandoned and very much on his own.

So as time passed and it approached the noon hour he decided to become proactive. He knew where Hakim Abdula lived. He felt that he was the key. He'd tail Abdula and try to find out for himself what was going on.

He never liked stakeouts. He'd rather do paperwork than sit on his duff, staring, watching and waiting. But here he was, sitting in his unmarked car, in the South Hills Village parking lot, one of Pittsburgh's biggest malls, watching the Abdulas. And what were they doing? They were sitting in their SUV, two rows away, doing what appeared to be the same thing, sitting and waiting. The tail had been short and uneventful. The Abdulas lived three minutes from the mall. As a matter or fact, you could see their house from where they were parked.

"Now what?" Caputo thought. He could arrest the two of them, but he knew that wouldn't break up the cell. It might even force them to initiate a backup plan that could end up being more devastating. No. He would have to be patient. He'd have to wait and hope for a better time when they could ensnare the entire group. He knew that patience was a virtue, but it was one virtue that he didn't possess.

"What were they doing?" he wondered. They appeared to be animated and in some kind of loud conversation. And it went back and forth. First Hakim would wave his arms and make pointed hand gestures and then Dana would appear to counter his movements.

After a period of time, their passionate conversation appeared to end and the two people appeared to calm down. Then for the next several minutes they simply sat. Hakim seemed to occasionally look down at his watch.

"What are you doing?" Caputo asked out loud, to an empty car.

Then, after several minutes of this, Caputo could see Hakim take out his cell phone and look over at his wife, as if for some kind of acquiescence. From a distance, her body language seemed to suggest that she was considering something. Then Caputo saw her nod her head, in what appeared to be approval.

Hakim punched in a set of numbers and hit the send button, but Caputo thought it was odd that he didn't bring the phone to his ear.

Suddenly there was a tremendous explosion and Caputo instinctively looked to the direction of the sound. Pieces of the Adbula's house were still sailing into the sky, as was a large billowing cloud of smoke.

"Holy shit!" was the first thing that he could say and that didn't come from him for at least thirty seconds. The surprise explosion had been so loud and powerful it had completely stunned the detective. He had lost the first half-minute of his life after the blast.

Then he realized what had happened. Hakim's phone call had triggered the explosion. Caputo looked back but the space where the Abdulas had been parked was empty. The car and the couple were gone.

"Oh man!" was all that Caputo could say as he pulled the car into gear and accelerated in the direction of where he hoped the Abdulas had gone.

But they hadn't. He had spent fifteen minutes driving around the area trying to find some trace of the couple, but to no avail. It was as if they had vaporized in thin air.

Once he accepted the fact that he had lost them, Caputo drove back to what had once been the Abdula's home. By the time he arrived, fire trucks and emergency vehicles were on the scene and had encircled the property. What he saw was the complete and total destruction of the Abdula house. Even the foundation of the house was demolished, which left the detective to conclude that the explosive device detonated in the basement.

It must have been a huge bomb to have left such a large crater. Neighboring homes, on all sides, were severely damaged. One was still burning. Caputo had been in gunfights and street battles but he had never experienced war. But he had seen the pictures. This scene looked like the remnants of war. Since 9-11 there had been a lot of talk and rhetoric about the 'war on terror', but for the first time he realized that the front lines of this battle were going to be a lot closer to home.

Kane poured some coffee and turned to Caputo. "I didn't intentionally leave you behind. As a matter of fact, I had planned on making the trip solo."

"I forced myself on the man. I force myself on every man," Sandy said with a coquettish smile.

Kane walked to his desk and sat down. "Anyway, it sounds as if your little sojourn was more exciting than ours."

"They blew up their damned house! What's that all about?" Sandy asked.

"Now there's no going back," Caputo said without hesitation. "The game's afoot."

"Do you think they went to the warehouse?" asked Sandy.

Caputo shook his head. "No. I checked it out on the way back. It's all locked up."

"Tell her the good part," Kane prodded.

It wasn't until he ran his hand over his face that Caputo realized that he had forgotten to shave. "All the trucks were gone."

Sandy looked a bit confused. "What do you mean gone? There were at least six big trucks in the parking lot."

"Well, they're not there anymore."

"And if I remember correctly, they were tanker trucks," Kane added.

"You have a good memory," Caputo said.

"When is the President due to arrive?" Kane asked.

Sandy shuffled through some papers on her desk, found what she was looking for and said, "He's scheduled to be at the podium, in the convention center, at 6 p.m."

"And what about the Israeli Prime Minister?"

"He's to speak just before the President. He'll be sitting on stage when the President delivers his speech."

Kane took a deep breath. "Great." He didn't mean it.

"Why the hell didn't they call this damn trip off?" Caputo asked, already knowing the answer.

"Both of these men refuse to be intimidated by terrorists," Kane replied.

"Yeah, but they're not invincible," Sandy said. "There aren't enough Secret Service agents in this country to protect them from a determined band of fanatics."

The room became quiet for a moment, as the three people seemed to consider their options.

"What about your friend in Washington?" Caputo asked Kane.

"I called him a few minutes ago. He's in as much of a tizzy as we are!"

"What about his operative here?"

Kane considered the question and then responded. "Damnedest thing!"

"What's that?" asked Sandy.

"Apparently just after we left the guy, Langley decided to terminate his involvement in the operation. They hadn't heard from him and they were uncomfortable with the infrequent communication. Well, to make things worse, now they can't get a hold of him at all."

"What do you mean? We were just there talking to him!"

"No one's answering the phone at the condo or his company cell."

"That's not good," said Caputo.

"He was on edge, don't you think?" Sandy said to Kane.

"Yeah, but he's a trained agent. No matter what, he'd never be totally incommunicado."

"So what do we do?" Caputo asked.

"We assume the worst. They either snatched him or he's dead."

"Dead?" said Sandy. "You really think that's a possibility?"

"Absolutely. You know that there are procedures. If they can't reach him, he can't be reached. Something very bad must've happened between the time we left him and now."

And as if by clockwork, Kane's cell phone rang. He was quick to answer it.

"Jack Kane," he said and then he listened intently. Caputo and Ryan sat starring at him as he listened.

"I knew it wasn't good," Kane said to the caller. "Thanks for the heads up."

Slowly he closed the flip phone and slipped it into his pocket.

"What's up?" Sandy asked.

Kane looked across at her and answered. "They found our friend in his doorway with a bullet hole in his forehead."

"No shit!" was all Caputo could say.

"So they were on to him," Sandy continued.

Kane stood up, coffee cup in hand and walked to a window.

"Why did they wait until now to kill him?"

"What do you mean?" asked Caputo.

He was looking out the window but he wasn't seeing anything beyond the glass. "They could've popped him a lot sooner. Why wait until now?"

Sandy looked down at her desktop and then back to Kane.

"Who knows what these people are thinking?"

"I don't understand why they waited. Why not take him out right away?"

"It could be that they just put it together," Caputo said.

Kane shook his head. "I don't know. It seems too coincidental if you ask me."

Sandy smiled. "That old gut instinct surfacing again, huh Jack?"

Kane turned back to his associates and placed the coffee cup down on the windowsill. "I never had much of that even when I was on the job. I always had to work at it. I saw a few guys get killed because of their gut instinct."

Caputo still had a hand to his unshaven face. "So let's see, if I've got this right; our suspects have blown up their home and killed one of our agents all within the last couple of hours."

"And we're still walking around with our heads up our asses," Kane furthered the hypothesis.

"Well gentlemen, we haven't got any more time to waste. We have to take the initiative. We have to make a plan based upon what we know to this point, don't you agree?" Sandy said as she tossed some papers into a wastebasket next to her desk.

Kane looked over at Sandy. "I agree. The problem is that we really don't know much, do we?"

"No we don't," Caputo concurred.

"We know who the local players are," Kane looked frustrated, "but we don't know where they are."

"We know that this Ghost character is a player, but we don't know why," Caputo added.

"Well, we can assume that it's for the money, but you're right, we don't really know for sure," said Kane." And we haven't got time to run around chasing any of these guys individually. We've got to protect the President and attack the group as a whole."

Sandy leaned forward in her chair. "So where do we begin?"

Kane thought for a moment and then answered, "Sandy, you've got to stay here and use your FBI connections to try to stop the President from going to that convention."

"Wow!" Sandy seemed overwhelmed. "I don't know, Jack. Sure, I have friends in Washington, but I don't know if they've got enough clout to stop the President from making this speech."

Caputo stood up. "How about your contact, Jack?"

Kane looked over at his friend. "He's doing everything that he can, trust me. But we can still use Sandy's contacts, too."

"I'll do everything that I can Jack, although I've got to tell you, I'm not crazy about sitting around the office while you two are out trying to catch the bad guys."

Kane walked over to Sandy and put a hand on her shoulder. "If you can stop the President from going into that convention center, then you're the hero here. We'll be checking in and we'll always be as close as the phone. I'll keep pressing Galego at the CIA to use his influence."

He looked to Caputo who said, "Where do we go?"

"We can try and stop him at the airport."

"They won't let you on the base," Sandy said.

"Not even with our credentials?" Kane asked.

Caputo grabbed his coat. "She's right. That airbase will be sealed off tighter than a drum."

Kane started for the door. "Well, then the next logical place is the convention center. Good luck with your friends in Washington."

Sandy lifted the phone from the receiver, "I'll need it."

Kane and Caputo left the room. Sandy had the phone next to her ear as they closed the door and were gone.

Sandy waited for a moment and then returned the phone to its cradle.

"What are we waiting for?" Caputo asked Kane. "I mean, I like the parking lot, the car's nice and you're, well, you're okay. But what's up? I thought we had to race to the convention center?"

"We do, Tom. In good time," Kane said as he looked across the parking lot to the federal office building and the door they had just used. "I'm just playing a hunch."

A few minutes passed and the door opened and Sandy appeared.

"Damn!" was Kane's initial response.

"Wait! What's Sandy doing? I thought she was going to work the phone and her Washington contacts!" Caputo said.

They watched the woman walk across the parking lot and get into her car.

"I guess I do have that old gut instinct," Kane said.

Caputo, who had been slouched in the seat, sat up. "Oh Jack, you can't be thinking what I think you're thinking!"

"If you think I'm thinking that she's one of the bad guys then you're thinking is right on the money," Kane said, still watching what the woman was doing.

Sandy started the car, pulled it into gear and accelerated out of the parking lot. Jack and Tom waited for a moment and then followed her.

"Gee, Jack, you can't really believe that Sandy's working against us!" Tom was having a hard time accepting the premise.

Jack may have been retired but his driving skills were as good as they had ever been. He paced Sandy's car, matching her move for move, without getting too close. Whenever he sensed that he might be detected, he backed off, sometimes to a point where Caputo thought that Kane had lost her.

"How well do you know Sandy?" Jack asked.

Tom took a moment.

"Actually, I don't know her very well at all. She just took this posting a few weeks ago."

Kane was focused on Sandy's car. "Where did she come from?"

"She said that she had been working out of headquarters in Washington."

Kane shook his head and sighed. "She said that she didn't have friends with clout there! She's supposed to be a senior field agent with thirteen years experience. If she is who she says she is, then she should have some friends with clout in the home office."

"Come on Jack, you can't judge her on just that! I've been a cop longer than she's been on the job, I worked in our headquarters, and I don't think that I have a lot of connections with the top brass either."

Sandy's car turned on to the parkway and Kane followed right along.

"I don't want to be right, Tom. I'd like to think that she is who she says she is but," there was sadness in his voice, "I don't think that she is."

It was almost too much for Caputo to comprehend. He was watching her car too, as it sped down the highway.

"What about her neighbor, Jack? Her neighbor's dead," Caputo said.

Kane didn't respond but his non-answer was answer enough.

"Oh wait, you don't think that.... She couldn't have!"

The two men traveled, for a time, in silence. Sandy's car turned off the Parkway East, at the Churchill exit, and they followed. The woman and her pursuers continued through the suburbs until they faded into an older section of town called Turtle Creek. Once a prosperous, steel producing section of Pittsburgh, Turtle Creek had become little more that a ghost town, littered with cavernous structures that were once giant steel mills and company warehouses. The dilapidated buildings were now nothing more than empty shells; the last vestiges of enormous old steel companies that had long since disappeared from the landscape of American industry.

"Where the hell is she going?" Caputo asked.

Kane slowed the car a little, careful not to drive too close to Sandy's vehicle that had slowed, too.

"I don't know, but she does."

"Man, you think you know people..." Caputo left the sentence unfinished.

The two-car procession drove by the Woodland Hills Junior High School, in the center of the small hamlet and continued along mill row, which lined the shore of Monongahela River.

"Do you think we should play dumb and call her cell phone?" Caputo asked.

"Yeah. Why not?"

Caputo took out his cell phone and punched in some numbers.

"I'm calling her office phone first, to leave a caller ID time stamp so we can say we tried the office first and then called her cell."

Kane grinned. "Smart thinking."

After a few rings he ended the call and entered in a new set of numbers. She answered on the second ring.

"Sandy Ryan," she said, sounding important.

"Sandy! Tom Caputo. I thought you'd be calling your contacts back in the office!"

"I made some calls after you guys left but I couldn't reach anyone. I thought I'd run over to my house for a few minutes. Are you guys at the convention center yet?" "Yes, we're parked about half a block away. We just got here," Tom lied. "Are you heading back to the office when you're done?"

Sandy's car slowed and turned into the entrance to, what looked to be, an abandoned forging mill.

"Yes," she said easily. "I'll probably get back to the office just after lunch. But remember, if you need me I'm as close as my cell phone."

Caputo looked over at Kane and shook his head. "And we are, too. Talk to you later."

There was a polite 'goodbye' and the conversation was over.

Slowly, Caputo closed his flip phone and slipped it into his coat pocket.

Kane parked just outside of the mill entrance in a spot that gave him a good view off the roadway and the lot where Sandy had stopped her car. She was still inside the vehicle.

"She said she was at her townhouse." Caputo's eyes were locked on the woman's car.

"Well, at least now we know that she's a liar." Kane said.

"I would have bet my life…"Caputo was still having a hard time accepting the facts.

"I think we may have been doing just that," Kane said as he looked into his rear view mirror. Suddenly a car appeared from behind. "Get down!"

Without hesitation, the two men ducked down in the seat, just before the car passed by their location and then turned into the mill entrance. Slowly, they peaked over the dashboard and saw that the threat had passed. Carefully they returned to their positions. Kane reached across the car, opened the glove compartment and took out a small pair of binoculars. He turned again toward Sandy and the stranger, put them to his eyes and adjusted the focus.

"What are they doing?" Caputo asked.

"She's out of the car and she seems to be waiting for the guy in the other car to do the same."

Kane made some more adjustments on the focus and then he saw the man get out. He leaned into the binoculars, as if trying to get a better look at what he was seeing.

"Well I'll be a son of a bitch!"

"What? What's happening?" Caputo said excitedly.

Kane, still looking into the glasses, didn't answer right away but then said, "The Ghost, I think she's meeting with the Ghost!"

"You've got to be kidding!" was all Caputo could say.

"Yup, that's him, missing finger and all."

"She knows that son of a bitch!" Caputo said.

Sandy walked to the man, embraced and kissed him.

"I'd say that they were even closer than that."

Caputo leaned forward, too, squinting to get a better look.

"Is she kissing the prick?" There were equal measures of anger and incredulity in his voice.

"Yeah, that's exactly what our friend is doing."

"Well what do you think? Shouldn't we just go in there and get the bastards?" Caputo sounded ready for action.

"Tom, if we go in there now we may blow the opportunity to stop the attack. We'd get these two runs and lose the game!"

Caputo slumped back in the seat. "So what the hell do we do? We just watch these two creeps get away?"

Kane was still looking through the glasses. "No, we just keep watching. They're not going to get away."

"To think, you could be back in New York enjoying your retirement."

"I've never had so much fun!" Kane said with a smile.

Sandy's conversation with the Ghost was becoming animated.

"Looks from here like it's getting a little hot over there," said Caputo.

"One of the little tricks of the trade that I picked up in my service to the CIA was reading lips," said Kane.

"You're kidding!" Caputo sounded amazed.

"Nope. It came in very handy on surveillance just like this," Kane said. "She just said that she's not happy with the way this is coming down. 'Things are getting too hot back at the office', she said."

"You think it's getting hot back at the office?" Caputo seemed to be evaluating that remark. "I don't. If you ask me, it's anything but hot back there. I mean I had no clue that she was one of the bad guys."

"I only began to get a bad feeling last night," Kane said.

"You did?"

"Yeah."

"I missed it altogether. I thought she was as American as apple pie and ice cream," Caputo continued. "What would make a kid like her do something like this?"

Kane leaned back from the binoculars and answered, "Only one thing."

"What's that?"

"She's not the kid she's pretended to be. She's as much of an operative as the Abdulas. She's a plant, too. She's a piece of their terror machine."

Kane resumed looking into the field glasses.

"You know, I think she's getting pissed at the guy," Kane observed.

"Based on his track record, that's not a good thing," said Caputo.

"Her arms are moving all over the place and she seems to be yelling."

"What's he doing?"

Kane took a moment before he answered, "Nothing. He's just standing there, looking like a hen-pecked husband."

The two men looked to each other, coming to the same conclusion simultaneously.

"Oh man. Here I thought the Ghost dude was a free wheeling operative like James Bond and in reality he's been domesticated."

Kane smiled. "Can you believe it? She's probably married to the jerk!"

"What else is she saying?"

"Let's see. She wants to know why the delay, whatever that means. And, I knew it."

"What?" Caputo said impatiently.

"And she just said that she took care of Mohammed Khan, a.k.a. agent Joe Silvia. Damn!" Kane said angrily. "I drove her to that poor guy's house."

Caputo put his hand on Kane's shoulder. "You couldn't have known. It's not something you did intentionally."

"Yeah, but I took her right to the door."

"Jack, she killed him, not you. When do you think she did it?"

Kane took a second to review the visit in his mind and then said, "When she went back for her purse."

"Her purse?"

"Yeah, just as we were pulling away she said that she left her purse back in Silvia's house. She asked me to stop and said she'd be right back. She wasn't gone three minutes, and she was cool as a cucumber. She must have shot him as soon as he opened the door."

"You didn't hear the gunshot?"

"No. She had to use a silencer. I didn't hear a thing. She got back into the car as if nothing had happened. You would never have suspected that she had just shot the top of a guy's head off."

Caputo winced as if what he was about to say was painful.

"Jack, can this really be our Sandy? I mean she's an FBI agent for crying out loud! How could she have infiltrated the damned Federal Bureau of Investigation?"

"She was probably an agent when she met this guy. Love and money make people do the strangest things."

"But the killing!" Caputo still sounded unconvinced.

"Who knows how long she's been at this? They say that it gets easier after the first time. Money, the belief in a cause, or love can make any action palatable." Kane was still looking at the couple in the parking lot. "I'll bet she killed her neighbor."

"You think?" Caputo replied. "But why?"

"She probably saw them together," Kane continued. "There wasn't a lot of blood splatter. The wounds didn't appear to be deep and there was absolutely no sign of forced entry. She knew her assailant. It had to be her."

"God, she apparently kills with ease," Caputo said to his partner.

"She's completely involved in this operation. She's going to disappear when this is over, you watch. And you can bet that she's never going back to the office. She's done with the ruse, and us. That's why she's here. She wants to be a part of the action. "

"Well let's go get the two assholes!" Caputo said impatiently.

"No. We can't jump the gun. They're going to lead us to the action."

"I don't know how you can do it Jack. I mean, they're right there. All we have to do is scoop them up."

"Patience, Tom. All in good time. I want them, too, and we'll get them, but we can't lose sight of the bigger picture."

Caputo sighed deeply. "Yeah, right. It's just so damn hard to let them go."

"We're not going to let them go. We're just giving them a little more rope to hang themselves."

"Her arms are still moving all over the place. She must really be giving him a piece of her mind."

"No, actually she just said that she's not going back." Kane lowered the binoculars. "She said that she wants to be the one to kill the President."

"Wow!" Caputo said. "She could just not vote for the guy."

Kane smiled and looked into the glasses again. "He just asked her how I was getting along and she said that I'm not slowing the case down as much as they had expected!"

Caputo smiled. "You mean that those jerks thought that you'd slow down the process?"

"I guess."

"They don't know you very well, do they?"

"I think they thought that my involvement would complicate our end. They'd have to get me up to speed. That would take time and some of our resources. I love it when my opponent underestimates me. Okay, I think the meeting's over."

"Is she going with him?"

"That's what it looks like. Why don't you try calling her cell again?"

Caputo pulled out his cell phone and dialed in her number. Kane continued to look through the glasses. Sandy and the Ghost had started to walk to his car when she stopped, took out her company cell phone, dropped it to the ground and crushed down on it with her foot.

"Do you know what she just did?" Kane asked.

"I could see that without the glasses."

"I would venture to say that our relationship with Sandy is officially over," Kane said.

"Yeah, I'd say that that's a good bet."

When they reached the Ghost's car, he reached through the window and took something off the front seat.

"What's he up to now?" Caputo asked.

Kane took a moment and sized the situation up through the glasses. "I think he just reached in and took out a two way radio. Now he's talking into it."

"What's he saying?"

"I can't tell. He's got his back to me."

Then there was a loud rumbling noise and some large steel doors, on the front of the old building they were standing near, began to rise.

"Well, what's this?" Kane said.

"I don't think they're alone."

A minute later the first huge tanker truck rolled through the open door.

"I think we'd better find a better vantage point. Those trucks are going to come this way and I don't want them rolling right over us," Kane said, as he pulled the gearshift into 'drive' and accelerated their car away from the entrance. He drove down the road another half block, pulled a u-turn to the other side of the street and stopped. Now he couldn't see Sandy and her boyfriend, but they still could see the mill entrance. They positioned themselves just in time to see the big tanker truck pass through the front entrance and turn away from them. A few seconds later the second big truck followed.

"Well, we know where the trucks are." Caputo said.

"Yeah, but where are they going?" Kane asked as the trucks continued to pull out of the mill site. After a few minutes, the last of the convoy exited the area and things became quiet again. The two men waited for a moment. Nothing.

"Where's the lovely couple?" Caputo asked.

"You got me! I think we'd better find them."

"What about the trucks?"

"They shouldn't be hard to find. Call it in and have them followed."

"I hate to think what they're going to do with those rigs," Caputo said as he dialed headquarters.

Kane eased the car forward again and stopped at the entrance. Both cars were still in the parking lot and the garage doors were closed.

"Where the hell are they?" Kane seemed puzzled.

He turned the car into the entrance, slowly drove to the two parked cars and stopped. There was no sign of the couple.

"I don't know. I didn't see them in the trucks, did you?" he asked Caputo.

"No. I only saw a driver in each cab."

"Then they've still got to be here."

He drove the car to the abandoned mill entrance and turned off the motor.

"We'd better check it out."

The two men got out of the car, weapons drawn and walked to a service entrance. Caputo pulled on the handle and to his surprise it was unlocked. Cautiously, he opened the door. They paused. It was absolutely quiet. There was no noise whatsoever.

"I don't like this." he whispered to Kane.

They moved into the old building and both men were immediately struck by its incredible size.

"We'll never be able to search this place. It's bigger than an aircraft carrier."

Kane agreed. "It's like a skyscraper on its side."

Caputo moved in a little more, looked around and stopped.

"You know, as big as it is, I think this place is empty."

Then Kane noticed a door on the other side of the warehouse that seemed partially open.

"We might want to see where that takes us," Kane said pointing to the opened door.

Slowly they walked across the cavernous room, looking all around as they made their way. They stopped at the door and Kane pushed it open the rest of the way. That was when he heard the noise of a boat engine.

"They're using a boat!" he said to Caputo.

The area behind the mill was overgrown with trees, wild shrubs and weeds. There were abandoned equipment and vehicles in disrepair. And just beyond, much louder now, was the sound of a boat motor powering up and moving away from the shore. Caputo and Kane ran toward the noise just in time to see the boat racing up river towards Pittsburgh, the Ghost and Sandy Ryan on board.

"Son of a bitch!" Caputo yelled.

Just then Khalil Rasheed stepped from behind a nearby stack of crates and fired a shot that narrowly missed hitting Caputo in the head. Kane's reaction was surprisingly quick and instinctive. He spun toward the sound of the gunshot and fired off four quick rounds, two of which hit the terrorist in the center of his chest, killing him instantly. He looked back to Caputo who was so completely surprised that he hadn't even had time to raise his weapon.

"Are you all right?" Kane asked.

"Yeah! Thanks for covering my back."

The two men turned again to the boat. It's distance from shore and the roar from the engine had completely blocked out the sound of the gunshots. The Ghost and Sandy were still looking in the direction of the city and were unaware of the gunfight.

"You'd better get some black and whites out here. They'll want to go over this place with a fine tooth comb."

"In the meantime we've got the President to worry about. Those two are headed toward the city," said Caputo.

"You're right and we've got to haul ass into town," Kane said, already moving in the direction of their car.

Chapter Fifteen

Two of the tanker trucks were stopped without incident. Both had been victims of a Pittsburgh rush hour traffic jam and the drivers had been apprehended quickly and quietly. Given the chance, they would have initiated their suicide option, that being self immolation along with the flammable contents of their trucks. But the arresting officers anticipated this and were upon them before they had the chance.

Three other trucks were also stopped before they reached their assigned destinations. One had turned on to a ramp that led to the Parkway North, but three city police cars that blocked the exit stopped its access. A team of police officers, firing high powered assault weapons, shot out several of the truck's tires and placed multiple rounds into the engine block, causing it to jackknife into and over the guardrail. The cab hung precariously over the side of the ramp. The trapped driver seemed dazed and confused. The police knew that they could not approach the truck until they were sure that the driver was going to surrender or that he was dead. The wait wasn't long. After only a few minutes, the desperate man yelled a short praise to Allah, triggered a device from within the cab, sparking a small explosive charge that had been placed directly under the center of the huge fuel tank. The big rig jumped and then buckled in a large and extremely powerful ball of flame. The fireball raced up the ramp and scorched the police cars that protected the patrolmen who we crouched down on the other side. The ramp was an inferno. Burning fuel shot out of every nook and cranny. Ribbons of fire dripped from the ramp down to the street below. Cars swerved to avoid the flames and nearby pedestrians ran for their lives. Fire crews responded quickly and, considering what they had to deal with, extinguished the fire in relatively short order. The threat from this truck was over. When the smoke cleared, the only life lost was that of the suicide driver.

Another of the trucks tried to escape from a small fleet of Pittsburgh police cars, by attempting to pull a U turn across a highway median, while traveling at sixty miles an hour. It wasn't a good plan. The top-heavy rig leaned hard to one side and then flipped over, ejecting the driver from the cab and then rolling over him. It slid across to the opposite side of the highway and slammed to a stop against a concrete barrier. When the dust settled and the wheels stopped spinning, the fuel tank was holding fast and the explosive charge, which hadn't detonated, remained in place. The driver, however, had become al Qaeda road kill.

A well-placed bullet fired from a SWAT sniper rifle stopped the fifth truck. The officer, who was perched on a walkway that spanned Pittsburgh's Parkway Central, squeezed off one shot and put the round through the windshield and directly between the driver's eyes. The driverless truck swerved to the left and slammed into the guardrail. The big machine scrapped along, disintegrating the front end, until abruptly hitting a concrete barrier.

Five of the deadly trucks had been quickly neutralized. But there was a problem. The sixth tanker was still missing. It was the rogue bull, nowhere to be found. Law enforcement from Pittsburgh and surrounding communities were conducting a widespread and intensive search but were having little success. No one had to be reminded that the detonation of even one well-placed fuel truck would be devastating.

Hakim and his wife, Dana, waited patiently at a boat landing across the Allegheny River from the David L. Lawrence convention center.

Hakim checked his watch. "Where the hell are they? They should be here by now."

"Patience my husband," Dana replied. "They're not late. They still have time."

Then Hakim's cell phone buzzed.

"Yes," he answered. "Where are you? Are you running on schedule?"

He listened and seemed pleased with their answer.

"We're here and we're ready. The trucks should be in place. All we need to do now is to place the package. Get here as quickly as you can."

He looked at his watch again and then over to the convention center, which seemed a buzz with activity. Of course with the pending arrival of the President of the United States and the presence of the Prime Minister of Israel, this was to be expected.

Hakim put his field glasses to his eyes and looked toward the Point, the place where the Monongahela and Allegheny Rivers meet to form the Ohio River. After a moment, a speeding boat appeared from around the Point and turned up the Allegheny toward their location.

"That's them." You could here the excitement in Hakim's voice. "It's time."

It was late in the afternoon and the sun was disappearing behind the ridge known locally as Mt Washington. Although there was still daylight, it had become dark enough for some cars to turn on their headlights.

"We have to be quick about this, Dana. Remember what we have to do?"

"We've discussed this a thousand times, Hakim. You just said yourself that everything's in place. We all know what has to be done. The package is almost here. We'll place and arm it and then we'll make our escape. When it goes off, we'll be long gone and America will have suffered a mortal wound," she smiled. "It is what we have worked for, for eight long years. It is our shared dream."

Abu Mirad stepped out of the shadows. His assignment was to guard Hakim.

"How much more time Hakim?" He was nervous. "The longer we wait here, the better our chance of being spotted. The Secret Service has been patrolling the area."

"And we'll keep avoiding them until we're absolutely ready to make our move," Hakim said firmly.

"But Hakim…"

"Enough, Abu." Hakim raised his hand to silence the man. "Today we all do what we have to do. You keep an eye out for the patrols and leave the rest of the decision making to me."

Abu was a loyal cell member. He knew who was in charge. He bowed his obedience and walked back to his post.

Hakim turned back to Dana. "I don't blame his nervousness. I'm as nervous as Abu. Something seems wrong. The whole process seems bogged down."

Dana tried to reassure Hakim again. "You're just concerned because the moment we've all been waiting for has arrived. Now that it's here, it's not happening fast enough. You're like a child impatiently waiting to go to the circus. Relax, Hakim. Rest assured that it's happening and it's happening now."

Hakim thought about what she had said and nodded in agreement. He looked back toward the approaching boat but, to his surprise, it had disappeared!

"What the hell!"

Dana stepped closer to her husband. "What's the problem Hakim?"

He seemed to pull the binoculars closer to his eyes.

"He was just there a second ago!"

"What do you mean?"

"He's gone. The boat is not there anymore!"

"Are you sure that it was the right boat?"

"I'm positive. Hell, it's my boat. I picked it out, bought and paid for it! I should know what the damn thing looks like!"

Then to his relief the boat reappeared from around a bridge piling, much closer now than he even expected.

"Praise be to Allah!" Hakim sighed.

Dana could see the boat without the field glasses.

"False alarm, thankfully," she agreed.

Hakim turned and motioned for Abu to come closer.

"The boat is here, my friend. It's time for the attack to begin."

Then the blare of sirens could be heard coming from the other side of the river. The startled Hakim quickly turned his glasses toward the sound, but when he saw the source of the noise, he smiled.

"The presidential motorcade. Our target has arrived." He looked down at his wristwatch. "Right on schedule."

Dana smiled. "Don't you feel better now, Hakim?"

"Yes, much better."

A couple of minutes later the Ghost and Sandy slowly pulled the boat into the dock and stopped.

"So, my dear, I guess you're now fully committed," Hakim said to Sandy.

Her demeanor was much different now that she was no longer playing the role of a dedicated FBI agent.

"I have always been fully committed," she said coldly. "You of all people should know that Hakim."

"Are you getting in?" the Ghost said impatiently. "I can't hold it here forever."

Hakim motioned for his wife to get in, which she did, and then Abu.

"There isn't enough room for him," the Ghost said firmly. "With the weapon on board, we only have enough room for you and your wife."

The unexpected problem surprised Hakim. "What do you mean? Why wasn't this discussed before now?"

"We have to take Abu. If we leave him here he will be caught for sure," Dana added.

Hakim became adamant, "No, no, he has to come with us. Get in Abu."

The bodyguard took a step toward the boat, as ordered.

"No, no, he can't," the Ghost said as he rapidly raised his silenced handgun and squeezed off two quick rounds into the man's chest. Abu staggered to the side and into the water.

The Ghost smiled. "Well, that settles that little problem."

Both Hakim and Dana stood dumbfounded.

"Well get in," he repeated. "We haven't got all day."

Slowly, Hakim stepped into the boat as instructed.

"Why did you do that?" he said in a low, almost soft voice.

The Ghost pulled back on the gearshift and the boat moved away from the dock.

"Knock it off, Hakim. You know that he was going to have to be eliminated sooner or later. You know that most of your cell members are loose ends. Your leader doesn't want any loose ends when this mission is completed."

"And he charged you with their removal?" Hakim asked.

The Ghost turned the steering wheel in the direction of the convention center.

"Among other things," he answered.

"Other things? What other things?"

"Have you seen our little package?" The Ghost pointed to a crate in the middle of the boat and totally ignored Hakim's question.

Hakim looked over at his wife, who was still in shock over Abu's murder, and then to the crate.

"So it's ready to go?"

"All set," the Ghost said almost cheerfully.

"And you know what to do?"

"Of course, my friend..."

"You sir, are most definitely not my friend," Hakim said angrily. "When this is finished I would suggest that you leave as soon as possible. You have created many new enemies and I would think that it would not be in your best interest to stay."

The Ghost smiled. "Oh, that sounds like a threat, Hakim. You wouldn't be threatening me would you?"

"Take it any way you'd like."

"Well, I live my whole life surrounded by enemies. Enemies are not a problem, Hakim,"

He paused for a moment and then turned directly to Hakim and finished his thought.

"It's some of my friends that I worry about." He looked back toward the front of the boat. Hakim was glaring at the mercenary.

Dana sighed and then seemed to pull herself together. "We have business to do here. What's done is done..What is important now is that we complete our mission."

"Your wife is a smart lady," the Ghost said unemotionally.

Hakim turned and fighting the boat's rocking movement, walked to the crate. He ran a hand over the box and seemed to examine it as if it were a new sports car. After a while, his thoughts returned to what was ahead of them.

"This will be big," he continued. "This will be very big."

He looked back and saw that the convention center was much closer now.

"You know where to dock the boat?" Hakim asked.

"Of course I do. We bring the boat in through the wharf supports that run under the riverside portion of the convention center. Then we dock near the maintenance access door that leads to the service area of the building."

"And then we break open this box and bring the toxin containers into the building," Hakim said, playing along. He knew that there were no toxin containers in the crate. He was well aware of the fact that they were about to detonate a suitcase nuke in the center of a major US city and that thought turned him on.

"Yeah, right." the Ghost said as he looked over to Sandy.

The Ghost idled down and the boat slowed as it went under the wharf and slipped through the darkness toward its destination.

"You know that there will be security down here. Sandy will flash her FBI credentials just long enough to confuse the agent, and just long enough for you to shoot him, Hakim."

"Me? Why me?" He was genuinely surprised.

"Because I'm not going to be the one that does all the killing on this mission. I've already gotten my hands dirty. Now it's time for you to get a little blood on yours. This isn't a problem, is it?"

"No," Hakim lied. He hadn't shot a man in nearly twenty years, when he was a younger man and lived in the Middle East. Killing is a much easier thing to do when you're young, he thought.

The Ghost reached into a bag, took out a Walther PPK 380 with a noise suppressor and handed it to Hakim.

"Aim carefully, my friend. You're not going to get a second chance."

Hakim was struck by the weight and balance of the precision weapon. It seemed custom made for his hand.

"We're close," Sandy said in a loud whisper. "Heads up everybody."

The boat moved around another cluster of large pylons that seemed critical to the support of the entire structure.

"This place is going to be a mess in a very short time," the Ghost said. "I'm glad I'm not going to be here when it goes off."

Suddenly a bright flashlight shined in their direction.

"Halt!" a voice commanded. "This is a secure area."

"I know," Sandy replied. She raised her FBI credentials into the light. "I'm with the bureau."

The beam lowered just enough for them to see that there wasn't one guard at this post, but two.

"Time for some improvisation, Hakim. You go for the one on the left," the Ghost said in a low voice. "You got it?"

"I've got it," Hakim answered as the boat continued to float closer.

"No one told us that the FBI was going to be down here!" the guard said.

"Are you sure?" Sandy seemed sincere. "Why don't you call your supervisor and see what he has to say."

"That's exactly what I'm going to do," he answered as he reached for the two-way on his belt.

"Now!" the Ghost ordered as he raised his gun, in unison with Hakim, and fired at precisely the same time.

Their accuracy was amazingly good. Both guards were hit in the head and killed instantly.

"Now that wasn't difficult, was it?" the Ghost said, seeming to savor the experience.

The moment was broken by Hakim.

"Put your gun down." He was pointing the Walther. The Ghost started to lower his weapon but then stopped and smiled.

"Now wait, my friend. Give me a second here." The Ghost took a breath and then continued. "Okay… so you know that I was going to double cross you. That's not a crate of toxic gas; it's a relatively unsophisticated but never the less quite effective nuclear bomb. Here's the catch. I know that you knew what I was going to do."

He paused and looked for a reaction from Hakim. To his surprise, there wasn't any.

"Hmmm. Well, do you remember that I told you that you'd better make your shot, that you'd only get one chance? That's because I only put one bullet in that gun."

Hakim looked down at the Walther.

"See, you didn't know that did you?" The Ghost seemed happy with himself.

Hakim looked back at the man. "Actually, I expected it."

He pulled another smaller handgun from his pocket.

"It's not as big, but from this range it'll do the job."

"Well, you are a man of many surprises Hakim. But you'd better hand me that gun right now."

"Or what, my friend?" Hakim asked sarcastically.

"Or I'll have to shoot you, my darling," Dana said from behind her husband.

Hakim turned quickly and saw that she was holding a small Beretta and it was aimed in his direction.

"What the..." was all he could say.

"I'm sorry Hakim. I love you, but I love our cause more. Our leader sent me specific instructions to back up the Ghost. I was told that he was in complete and total control and to do absolutely anything and everything he told me to do. He told me to cover him, and to watch you," Dana explained.

The Ghost gestured to the gun. "As I was saying, give me the gun Hakim."

He hesitated and then slowly handed the pistol to the Ghost. The killer took it with his free hand and then motioned to Dana to lower her gun. As she was doing so, he suddenly raised his gun and shot her dead. The bullet slammed into the middle of her chest, flipped her out of the boat and into the water.

"Women!" the Ghost said with disgust. Then he turned to Sandy, "No offense."

"None taken," she answered, seemingly unmoved by the entire incident.

"God man, if you can't trust your wife, who can you trust?" he said to Hakim who was still looking back at the place where his wife had been standing just a moment before. "You're now officially divorced."

"Why? Was the plan always that we would die?" Hakim asked, still back to the Ghost.

"Like I said before… no loose ends. Your entire organization is a loose end. My job is to make sure that everything goes off as scheduled, so to speak, and nothing is traceable.

Hakim turned back to the Ghost and Sandy. "What about her?"

"Let's just say that she's not a loose end and leave it at that."

"It's not going to work," Hakim said. "You've killed most, but not all of us."

"That's where you're wrong, I'm afraid. I take it you're referring to Ranoud."

Hakim's eyes widened. "What about him?"

The Ghost moved to a bench seat that ran along the side of the boat and lifted the cushion. Ranoud's lifeless body was stuffed tightly into the small space under the seat. "I have to admit he put up one hell of a struggle. I don't think he wanted to die. But in the end, a well placed knee to the neck, a quick jerk backwards and then to the side and it snapped like a wishbone."

The Ghost waited for a reaction.

"Why don't you just shoot me and get it over?"

The Ghost closed the bench seat and moved back to the front of the boat. "Because I have my orders."

"Your orders," Hakim said sarcastically.

"Yes, my orders and they are to make sure you're at your post and alert when the weapon is triggered."

"Why?"

"Because our leader wants you to die like a true soldier of Allah." The Ghost seemed to take pleasure in the words. "Not what you wanted to hear, old boy?"

Hakim looked down at the floor of the boat.

"You should be happy. Our leader knows that you'll be rewarded in heaven and that this is what you really want," he chuckled. "Hey man, when this goes off you're going to be propelled right into the afterlife. Wow! Just think of all those vestal virgins! You'll be too busy to miss that old hag wife of yours."

The Ghost pulled a set of handcuffs from his coat pocket and handed the gun to Sandy.

"If he makes one quick move, send him to Allah."

He grabbed Hakim, pulled him to the floor and handcuffed him to a heavy metal crate handle.

"What do you get out of this?" Hakim asked the Ghost.

"What I always get, a lot of money, and a fun time doing what I like to do."

He raised the cover on the crate and then the heavy lid on the metal box inside. Sandy stepped forward to get a better look at the bomb.

"I know… it doesn't look like much. It's not like those fancy bombs with all the blinking lights that you see in the movies, but it will do the job."

Sandy smiled as if she was looking at a fine piece of jewelry. "They say that it should kill eighty to one hundred thousand people. I'd say that that was doing the job."

"And you can kiss this renovated convention center, most of downtown and the two shiny new ballparks, good-bye," the Ghost added. He reached into the container, placed his finger on a button and then said, "Here goes." He pressed the trigger and a timer started to count down. "We've got a half hour, my dear, to get as far away from this place as possible."

Sandy looked at her watch. "Our timing looks perfect. The President should be speaking when this thing goes off."

"Now let's move." The Ghost jumped to the dock and then pulled Sandy up. He waved to Hakim. "Have a blast my friend."

"Go to hell," Hakim yelled.

"Probably."

Hakim yanked hard on the handcuff but it didn't budge.

He was stuck. He leaned back on the crate and for the first time he noticed the clicking noise that the timer made as it devoured the seconds and minutes. He took a deep breath. He resigned himself to the inevitable. The Ghost was right. In less than an hour he would be with Allah.

Chapter Sixteen

The city had been cordoned off nicely for the President's visit. Roadways that were normally bumper-to-bumper with rush hour traffic were basically empty. The only exceptions being the occasional city patrol car or state police vehicle. People were told to leave work early, which many did, or they'd have to stay in town and wait until the President left the city before the highways and bridges would be reopened. Kane and Caputo had no problem getting into the city. They exited the Parkway at the Grant street exit and used that road to cut across town to the convention center. They pulled their car onto the sidewalk near the front entrance and were immediately greeted by anxious secret service agents.

"What the hell are you doing?" one screamed. "You can't leave that there."

Caputo flashed his badge and then threw him the keys.

"You park it then."

The agent looked at the keys in his hand, as if he had just caught a handful of manure. He tossed them back to Caputo. "You're a cop! Well, then I guess it's okay."

Caputo looked at the smiling Kane and they both walked into the building.

"What would you have done if he took the keys and moved it?" Kane asked.

"That would have been a miracle."

"Why's that?"

"Because I gave him the keys to my desk."

Kane's smile widened.

Then they pushed the second set of entry doors open to a lobby filled with strange faces.

"My God, Jack. Where do we begin?"

Kane thought for a second.

"They came by boat. There has to be a door that leads to the river. That's where they've got to be."

"You don't think that they parked the boat down river and walked?"

"No. They haven't got enough time, not if they want to kill the President. No, the boat's got to be here."

"It's as good a place as any to start I guess," Caputo agreed.

They ran toward the river side of the building and along the way stopped a maintenance man who was carrying some folding chairs.

Caputo raised his badge again. "Is there an exit to the river?"

The man thought for a second and then said, "There's a maintenance door that leads down to a wharf that runs under the north wing of the building."

"A wharf!" Kane said.

"Yeah. We use it to service the undercarriage of that part of the building. It's the new part that hangs over the Allegheny."

"How do we get there?" Caputo asked nervously.

"Well you can't use it. It's locked."

"You've got keys, don't you?"

"Well yes but…"

"Give them to me."

The man hesitated.

"Now." Caputo ordered.

The maintenance man pulled a large ring of keys from his pocket and presented them to Caputo.

"Which one?"

He shuffled through a few until he found the right one.

"This one, I think," he said, handing it to Caputo.

"You think?"

He shrugged his shoulders.

"Why don't you come with us?" Kane suggested.

The man looked at the chairs. "But these…"

"They can stand until you get back," Caputo said.

The maintenance man placed the chairs against the wall. "Follow me."

The access door that led to the river was at precisely the opposite side of the building from where Kane and Caputo had entered the convention center. It was a long walk.

"Geez, I'm tired already," Kane said as he loosened the top button of his shirt. "I'm getting too old for this James Bond stuff."

"You love it," said Caputo.

"Yeah, I love it," but Kane didn't mean it.

The maintenance man turned a corner and they followed, just in time to meet the Ghost and Sandy, face to face. For a moment, neither couple knew what to do.

Then Sandy pulled out her badge, raised it above her head so that anyone nearby could see it, and yelled, "FBI - these two men are under arrest."

As if from out of nowhere, Secret Service agents appeared with their guns drawn and surrounded Kane and Caputo.

"These two men are to be arrested as a physical threat to the President," she screamed to a lead agent.

"That's bullshit," Caputo said as he reached for his credentials. This time, however, he was stopped when an agent raised his weapon as if to fire. The Secret Service personnel swarmed closer and within seconds Kane and Caputo were pinned against a wall. Kane looked over his shoulder in time to see Sandy and the Ghost walking away. The Ghost saw him and raised his middle finger in the universal salute. A short time later they disappeared into the crowd.

It took Caputo ten valuable minutes to convince the agents that they were not the bad guys and that they were running out of time. Kane, Caputo and the maintenance man resumed their trek but now an entourage of Secret Service agents accompanied them.

They had been given the correct key and were through the door, in short order and heading down a long flight of stairs toward the river. They pushed through a storm door at the bottom of the stairs and were outside, under the convention center, standing next to the Allegheny River.

"It has to be right around here," Kane said.

"What exactly are we looking for down here?" Caputo asked. "Didn't we just pass the crooks in the convention hall?"

"They were empty handed," said Kane. "Whatever they planted is down here."

Caputo looked around the big dark area. "Oh man, we've got our work cut out for us. It could take hours to search this place."

"We haven't got hours."

"Well then we'd better get started."

Then they heard, "Over here!" It was Hakim.

"Well I'll be damned," Caputo said as they arrived at the boat. "Where's the Mrs.?"

Hakim lowered his head and then looked back at the policeman. "She went for a swim."

"A swim?" Caputo didn't get it.

"They shot her. She's in there." Hakim nodded toward the river.

"Oh!" Caputo got it.

"They shot her and let you live! That's strange, don't you think?" Kane asked Hakim.

"They weren't doing me any favors."

Then Kane looked over at the crate.

"What's in the box?"

"A most terrible surprise." Hakim responded with a sardonic sneer.

Kane turned to Caputo who said, "I hate surprises."

Kane leaned to the box and placed a hand on the cover.

"Aren't you going to release me?" Hakim asked.

Kane turned to the terrorist. "You're right where you should be. If we can't stop whatever is in this box then I think you should be the first to experience this terrible surprise. What do you think, Tom?"

Caputo stepped into the boat.

"I'm with you, pal. Although if we can't stop this damned thing, I wouldn't mind cutting off his nuts and sending him to the hereafter as a eunuch," he said matter-of-factly."

Kane slowly lifted the box cover and revealed the metal container inside. The counter noise became louder and more pronounced.

"Oh man, I really should have caught another flight," Kane said. "Well, I guess I can't stop now, can I?"

He grabbed the metal lid with both hands and carefully lifted it open.

"My God," he sighed. "We've only got six minutes."

"What is it?" Caputo asked.

"It's a bomb."

"Yeah, but it doesn't look like your ordinary garden variety bomb, does it?"

"No, Tom. If I've got this right, it's some type of nuclear device."

The Secret Service agents took a noticeable step backwards when they heard that.

"Should we clear the convention center?" one agent asked.

Kane shook his head. "If this goes off, everybody can be on the other side of town and it'll still take them out. Besides, we don't need the panic."

"What about the President and Prime Minister?" another asked.

"Have you got a helicopter nearby?" inquired Kane.

"We have one in the air right now. It's circling the city. It's a standard precautionary measure."

"How soon can you get it here and get them on board?"

"Two or three minutes," the agent responded.

"Well then I'd suggest that you get on it," Caputo said. "But don't tell anyone why. We don't need a mob scene up there."

The agent pulled out his two-way and started barking orders as he ran to the door.

"Can you stop it?" Caputo asked Kane. "Because I don't know a damn thing about bombs. I missed that course at the academy."

Kane ran a hand over the top of the device.

"Anything I do will be an educated guess."

"Well I guess that will have to do because it'll take longer than six minutes for the bomb squad to get here."

"Five."

"What?"

"Now we only have five minutes," corrected Kane.

He ran both hands carefully along the sides of the bomb. A helicopter could be heard landing nearby.

"Is this one of those dirty bombs they're always talking about?" an agent asked.

"No, actually this is a little more sophisticated than that. I think we're looking at a genuine eighties era Russian made suitcase nuke," said Kane. "Smaller than the bomb that leveled Hiroshima, but large enough to take out this entire downtown area."

"Great," was all Caputo could say. "You think that maybe we should do something? I mean we're down to four minutes."

They all heard the helicopter engines, this time taking off and then moving away.

"Good. At least the President and Prime Minister are safe." Kane turned to Hakim. "What would you do?"

Hakim smiled, "Pray."

It was not the answer Kane was looking for. "Maybe you should cut off his nuts."

"I may do it even if we do stop his terrible surprise," said Caputo.

Kane found a cable that ran from the bottom of the bomb, through the base of the casing, along the floor to the boat's motor housing.

"Maybe we're going to get lucky," Kane said. "I think this cable runs to the boat's battery. It may be the power source."

"So rip it out!" Caputo suggested enthusiastically.

"Then again, doing that might set it off," Kane continued.

"We've got less than three minutes, Jack. We haven't got a lot of options."

"Isn't there an off button?" another agent asked.

Caputo turned to the man. "You really do work for the federal government, don't you?"

"It was the first thing I checked for," Kane said.

"Maybe the same button that starts it, stops it if you press it again," the agent theorized.

"Or maybe it will instantly vaporize us."

The agent swallowed hard and stepped back. He had no more suggestions.

"We're wasting time Jack. You might as well pull that friggin' cable."

Kane looked over at the counter. He couldn't believe how fast it was moving. Now he had less than a minute.

"Oh boy." His palms were unusually sweaty. He wiped them on his pants and took hold of the cable again. "Here goes."

He pulled hard on the wire and it sparked when it snapped away from the terminals. Everyone flinched, expecting the worst. Kane opened his eyes and looked at the counter. He had less than thirty seconds and it was still counting down.

"Damn!" he said.

"What?" asked Caputo.

"It didn't work." Kane sounded desperate.

His hands were nervously scanning the bomb's perimeter. Fifteen seconds.

"I don't like this," voiced Caputo.

Ten seconds.

"Oh, what the hell," Kane said just before he did what the agent suggested and pressed the triggering button again. To his amazement, it stopped, with three seconds left. Kane turned to the agents.

"Good suggestion. Now I would suggest that you clear this place and evacuate as much of the downtown area as you can until the bomb squad boys have permanently disarmed this bad boy."

The men turned and scrambled back up the staircase. Now it was just Kane, Caputo and Hakim.

Caputo turned to Hakim. "Well, I guess you get to keep your nuts for a while longer."

"Where did they go?" Kane said in a calm voice.

"How should I know?"

"Because you masterminded this entire thing," Kane explained.

"Do you really think that they're following my plan? I don't think so. My plan didn't include my being handcuffed to the bomb."

"He makes a good point, Jack," Caputo grinned.

Kane leaned closer to Hakim, "I think that this was a minor alteration. I think you were privy to most everything else."

Kane reached into his coat and took out his gun. He didn't point it at the man or wave it in a menacing way. He simply held it by his side. "Now let's not waste each other's time here, Mr. Abdula. Where do you think they went?"

"What? So now you're going to shoot me? Do you think that scares me? You don't scare me. Nothing about this godless country of yours scares me. The only thing I fear is not spending eternity with Allah." Then he shouted, "All praise is to Allah!" And he reached into the crate to press the button again.

"Give him my regards," Kane said as he raised the gun.

Hakim's finger was less than an inch away from the trigger when Kane placed his gun-barrel to the cell leader's temple and fired. He fell backwards and slumped to the floor, a contorted expression of death on his face.

There was silence for a minute and then Caputo said. "Okay then, well maybe next time we should close the cover before we start interrogating the terrorist."

"I agree," Kane said.

Caputo looked down at the body. "Boy, the guy sure didn't like us very much, did he?"

"What did we ever do to piss him off?" Kane asked.

Kane slipped his gun into its holster and then closed both covers.

"We've got to stop them, Tom. They're going to know that we stopped it from going off when they don't hear the loud bang and see that big mushroom cloud."

"Do you think they have a backup plan?"

"No. Right now they're probably running as fast as they can. I think they'll try to get away, hide and then regroup so they can try something like this again at another time."

"They may have been able to get out of town and away from the danger zone. They've had twenty minutes, maybe even a little longer. All they would have had to do is get through the Fort Pitt Tunnels and just keep driving. They could be ten miles away by now and Mount Washington would act as a natural protective barrier," Caputo said.

"You know, if it were me I'd head for Canada," Kane said.

"And the easiest way for them to do that would be to take the Parkway West to 79 North and just keep driving." the local cop said. "Ah, but we really have no idea what they're driving, do we?"

"No," Kane said. "They could be in anything and just about anywhere right now."

"Damn!" Caputo snapped. "We can't just stay here and do nothing."

Kane stepped out of the boat and Caputo followed. Just then the Pittsburgh Police bomb squad arrived.

"Okay guys, we'll take it from here," an enthusiastic officer said.

"Fine with me," Kane said, as he stood aside to let them by.

An officer pointed to Hakim's corpse. "What happened to him?"

"He tried to kill us."

"Handcuffed to the boat?" another said. "How?"

"By trying to detonate that bomb you're standing next to," Kane answered.

"I hope you guys have had a lot of training disarming suitcase nukes," Caputo said.

The group stopped en masse.

"It's a nuke?" one asked meekly.

"Relax," Kane said. "We turned it off."

"But you might want to get your best people in on this one," Caputo suggested.

The two men started to walk toward the stairs, but Kane stopped and turned back to the policemen. "Oh, whatever you do, don't press that button. If you do, your life expectancy will be shortened to just about three seconds." He turned and continued through the doors and to the stairs. He rejoined Caputo at the top of the staircase.

"Aren't you afraid that they're going to accidentally trigger the bomb?" Caputo was seriously concerned.

"Once I stopped the damn thing, I removed the firing pin."

"You did? I missed that!"

"It only took a second and it was easy," Kane smiled. "Everything's easier when you're not under the gun."

"Was that something they taught you in the CIA?"

"Among other things. Now we'd better get a move on."

"Wouldn't it be nice to know what we're looking for?"

"Maybe we'll get lucky."

"We may have used up all of our luck with that bomb back there."

"Yeah, you're probably right," Kane agreed. "To think that fingerless bastard got away again. That makes me want to puke."

"He's probably laughing his ass off right now."

They made good time getting to their car, but the city was snarled in a massive traffic jam. Everyone was trying to leave.

"You think this might have slowed them down too?" Caputo asked.

"I doubt it," Kane answered. "I think they got a head start on all this."

"Well, there are some advantages to being a cop," Caputo said as he turned on the car's flashing lights and swerved into the emergency lane. "This should get us around these happy people and through the tunnel."

They left Penn Avenue and started for the on ramp to the Fort Pitt Bridge when a frantic police officer stepped in front of their car and stopped them.

He ran around to the driver's side window. "You can't go through. You've got to back up."

"What's the problem?" asked Caputo, as he flashed his detective credentials.

"I'm sorry, sir, but we've got a situation with a couple of vehicles in the tunnel."

"A situation?"

"Yes," he went on. "We cornered one of those tanker trucks, you know, one of the six we were chasing this afternoon. Well, we've got him trapped in the tunnel."

"And the other car?" Caputo prodded.

"Well, some FBI chick came racing up here just a minute ago and she was all lights and siren too. She didn't even stop! She just slowed down, flashed her badge and kept on going. I didn't have time to stop her."

Caputo turned to Kane, "Maybe we have a little luck left after all."

Khaled Kabbani was confused. He sat in the cab of the big tanker truck trying to decide what to do. The thumb of his right hand kept tapping the trigger that would turn his rig into a powerful bomb. He was surprised that he hadn't done so automatically. He had been so confident when he volunteered for this assignment. All he had to do was place his truck, press the button and he'd be with Allah. Simple. Quick. Straightforward. But it wasn't as easy as he had thought. There was a part of him that didn't want to die.... a part that kept saying that there was more life to live. However, the other side kept reminding him of his duty, his responsibility to God. It was all so confusing, he thought. He looked out of the front of the cab and saw the police cars that blocked his exit. Why had it come to this? He tapped the switch again. How could he make this decision? It seemed to be so much for one man, too much for him. Then he glanced into his large side view mirror and saw a police car racing toward him. The siren and the flashing lights startled him. He didn't see the woman driver. All he saw was the approaching threat to the success of his mission. It was all happening so fast now. He tapped the trigger. He looked again and the car was much closer. They were coming for him. There could be no more vacillating. A decision had to be made. He said a quick prayer, flicked the safety cover up and then pressed the button.

It wasn't until she was well inside the tunnel that she realized what it was that was blocking the otherwise empty tunnel ahead. Sandy slammed on the brakes; her car fishtailed and screeched to a stop. She slapped the gearshift into reverse and pressed the accelerator to the floor, but it was too late. The explosion and fireball were massive and the force from the blast shot her flaming car out of the tunnel like a bullet fired from a high-powered rifle. It flew through the air, hit an abutment on the opposite side of the Fort Pitt Bridge and disintegrated upon impact. Mercifully, Sandy Ryan was dead long before that happened.

The Fort Pitt Tunnels were newly renovated and held up surprisingly well, considering the enormity of the explosion. The pressure from the blast was released through the openings, saving the tunnel from severe internal structural damage. The fire was extinguished quickly. The charred and smoldering remains of Khaled Kabbani's tanker truck were towed away to that unseen place where terrible things like this were taken.

Traffic, however, was still not being permitted to use the tunnel. Everything had to be checked and double-checked. Then there were the county and state engineers who had to sign off on the usability of the passageway. It would be closed for several hours more. Thousands of cars were re-routed to the West End and Liberty Bridges. People would be late getting home. What most of them would never know is how close they had all come to never going home again.

Kane and Caputo sorted through the pieces of what had been Sandy's car. Her remains had been examined on-site and taken to the morgue. The people in the cars that were already on the bridge and tunnel approach ramps were the real losers. They couldn't go forward and they couldn't back off the ramps. They were stuck and there for the duration.

Kane walked over and leaned against the bridge railing. After a minute or so Caputo joined him.

"Where is he?" Kane said. "They were together when we saw them in the convention center. Where is he now?"

Caputo surveyed the site. "He can't be too far from here. Do you think that he might have gotten out in the tunnel and escaped through an access door before the explosion?"

Kane shook his head. "He didn't have enough time. I think he would have been fried to a crisp. He had to get out before she blew by the guard. No, he wasn't in the car when she entered the tunnel."

"Why split up?" Caputo asked.

"No matter what their relationship may have been, for the most part the Ghost works alone. He survives on his independence and self-reliance. Other people slow him down and increase his risk of being caught."

"What was it with Sandy?"

"She was probably his girlfriend."

"They say love is blind," Caputo said.

"…and stupid," Kane added.

"I wonder if that slime ball has the capacity to love."

"I know what you mean. People like him are soul-less; they have no feelings. How can they truly love?" Kane asked. "She was a foolish woman and she paid the ultimate price for her foolishness."

"Let's walk down the ramp she drove up on and see if we can pick up on something," Caputo suggested. "I know it's a long shot, but who knows? We might get lucky."

"Why not?" Kane agreed.

The two men sauntered across the bridge and started down the ramp, walking by the many gridlocked vehicles. What a variety of cars and people, Kane thought. There were economy cars and SUVs, trucks, luxury sedans and even a bus. Some people seemed calm and resolved to the situation, others impatient and even angry. All weren't going anywhere.

Then, something caught Kane's eye. It was when he walked past the bus. Was the man who was reading the newspaper missing a finger? Did he see that or was his mind playing tricks on him? He turned back quickly to the bus.

"You see something?" asked Caputo.

Kane panned the bus windows, but this time he didn't see the man or a newspaper. Was it wishful thinking? He walked around to the other side. Still there was no newspaper and no man in the window.

"I could have sworn I saw a guy reading a newspaper."

"What?" Caputo sounded confused. "What's so special about a guy reading a newspaper?"

Kane turned to his friend. "He was missing a finger, his pinky finger."

Caputo pulled out his gun. "I think maybe we should take a look inside."

The two men cautiously approached the front of the bus and Caputo tapped on the door with the butt of his gun. The driver opened the door and his eyes widened when he saw the gun.

"What the hell's going on?" He sounded frightened.

"Relax." Caputo held out his credentials and the driver seemed to relax. "Did you pick up any strange characters in your last couple of stops?"

The driver smiled. "What? This is a Port Authority bus. I pick up strange characters at almost every bus stop."

"Yeah, well you might have noticed that this one was missing a pinky finger."

There was a look of recognition on the driver's face. "Oh, him! He just got on at Stanwix Street."

"Stanwix Street?" Kane wasn't familiar with the name.

"It's a couple of blocks from here. It was probably the last stop before the bridge," Caputo explained.

Caputo leaned in closer to the driver and asked in a low voice, "Where is he sitting?"

The bus driver looked up into his rearview mirror and scanned the passengers. It was a full bus and there were a lot of them.

"I don't see him!" He seemed surprised. "I swear that I just saw the guy a minute ago."

Caputo turned to Kane. "Jack, stay here. I've got to do this one myself."

Before Kane could protest, Caputo turned and entered the bus. When he stepped into the aisle, he raised his badge and announced to the passengers, "Hi folks, I'm detective Tom Caputo. I'm sorry to inconvenience you, but I'm looking for someone and he might be on this bus. I'd appreciate it if all the men would show me their hands when I walk down the aisle. This should take just a minute and I'll be out of your way before you know it."

"It's not like we're going anywhere," someone said and there was a small burst of laughter.

Caputo started his inspection looking from side to side at the array of hands. There were no hands with missing digits. He walked to the back of the bus and, satisfied that his inspection was complete, turned and started to walk back to the front. Halfway back he heard a click from the lavatory lock and then the sound of the door opening behind him.

"The bathroom! Shit!" he said as he started to swing around. Then he heard a gunshot and it felt as if someone had hit him in the backside with a baseball bat. Caputo fell to the floor. He still didn't believe that he had been shot.

The Ghost wasted no time. He knew that there was none to waste. He pulled the passengers from the back seat and in one powerful move, kicked out the emergency window. Without hesitation he jumped, feet first, through the opening. A moment later he was on the street. But something was wrong. The sharp pain in his right ankle hadn't been anticipated. He stood, and when he tried to walk the pain was excruciating. But he didn't have any other options. He had to walk on it. He had to get away.

As soon as he heard the gunshot, Kane had entered the bus. In a moment he was at his friend's side.

"Where are you hit?"

"I think he shot me in the ass!"

"You too!" Kane sounded amazed.

Caputo sat up on his good side. "Does he shoot all his victims in the ass?"

"I don't know. Maybe we're just lucky."

"I'm all right Jack. I'll radio for an ambulance. Go see if you can get the son of a bitch."

Kane didn't have to be asked again. He patted his friend on the shoulder and headed for the exit. He ran to the rear and around to the back of the bus but the Ghost was gone.

"Son of a bitch!" he yelled in frustration. Then he saw a small child in a car next to the bus, looking directly at him. His first reaction was mortification for swearing in front of the little girl. His Irish Catholic conscience surfaced and he believed instantly that God would strike him dead and send him straight to hell for fouling the ears of an innocent. But then he noticed her hand. She was pointing back toward the bridge. Then Kane got it.

"Did he go that way?" he asked the little girl. She nodded in the affirmative.

"Thanks sweetie," he said with a smile to the little girl, who returned the look to him.

Not including the bus, Kane was at least ten car lengths from the bridge. He realized that the Ghost had a decent head start. And if he remembered correctly, the Ghost was younger and in much better shape. The arthroscopic knee surgery Kane had had eight months earlier hadn't helped his chances of catching the Ghost either. But he moved as quickly as he could and he was surprised at how well he was actually able to maneuver. Halfway to the bridge he caught a glimpse of the Ghost. He was limping like John Wilkes Booth. He looked so lame that had he been a horse he surely would have been put down.

"Stop!" Kane yelled to the man.

The Ghost fired a wild shot that hit a railing and sailed into space. Kane ducked between two cars and waited for a moment. Right away, he realized that if the Ghost fired another shot, the bullet might hit someone in one of the cars or possibly on the bus. There would be no more yelling. Slowly, he stepped, from the position of safety, into the potential line of fire. The Ghost was almost on the bridge deck, but having a very difficult time making his escape. Even from this distance Kane could see that the man was dragging his fractured ankle behind him.

"You're not getting away this time, you bastard," Kane said out loud, but to himself.

Kane kept low and zigzagged through the parked cars until he, too, was on the bridge deck and now much closer to the Ghost, who was now nearing its center, on the eastern side of the span. Kane hurried across to the western side and ran from support to support until he was just across the roadway from the Ghost.

"Give it up," he yelled to the killer. The Ghost wheeled and fired four quick shots at Kane. He was a good shot. Two of the rounds hit within inches of Kane's head, one ricocheted just an inch from his face.

"This is going to have a bad ending," Kane yelled again to the Ghost.

"Yeah, for you," the Ghost yelled back and then fired another two shots in Kane's direction. Kane gambled a look and squeezed two shots off at his opponent.

"Owww!" he heard the Ghost yell.

Kane looked again and saw the Ghost grab his gimp leg, only this time higher, in his thigh area.

"Yes!" he whispered excitedly to himself. He had winged the Ghost and that would slow him down even more.

"You're not getting out of here!" he yelled again to the wounded man. "You're limping and wounded. Why don't you throw down your gun and come out?"

"Why don't you eat me?" the Ghost yelled back. A second later he fired another shot that seemed to hit even closer to Kane. Obviously, the killer's health concerns hadn't diminished his shooting capability. Kane took a breath and ran to another support with the hope of getting a better angle of the Ghost. His timing was perfect. He knew that the Ghost missed the move when the wounded man fired again at the location Kane had just abandoned. His new vantage point revealed even more of the man. Kane could see that the Ghost had paused to reload his gun. Kane took the opportunity to do the same. Then he waited and hoped for another lucky shot. He didn't have to wait very long. The Ghost raised his gun to take aim and Kane fired. It really was another incredibly lucky shot. He was firing across the width of the span! His bullet struck the Ghost's hand and the weapon flew from his hand.

"Shit!" yelled the Ghost. "What are you, friggin' Billy the Kid?"

Kane waited. He knew that the criminal probably had another weapon. Kane looked around the bridge deck again and noticed policemen running up the ramp toward their location.

"There's no where to go. In a second, there's going to be a dozen cops pointing their guns at you," Kane screamed. "Give it up!"

He peaked out from behind the bridge support in time to see the Ghost gingerly step over the railing. He was now standing forty feet above the Monongahela River.

"Wait!" Kane cried. "Don't do it."

The Ghost turned to Kane and gave him the coldest, most vindictive look the detective had ever seen, then turned back to the river and jumped.

"What the…" Kane didn't finish the sentence.

He ran across the bridge and leaned over the railing. All that could be seen, in the light of dusk, was fast moving, dirty brown water. There was no sign of the Ghost.

He turned, again, to run to the other side of the street and found a small arsenal of handguns pointing at his head.

"Drop it," someone ordered. "Slowly."

Kane didn't need to be told twice. There were too many nervous fingers pressing against the triggers of high-powered weapons that were aimed in his direction.

"I'm on your side, guys. Jack Kane, NYPD retired."

Then he heard a familiar voice.

"Relax fellas. He really is with us," Caputo said, holding a hand to his gluteus maximus. The policemen looked toward Caputo and then lowered their guns. One glanced down at the detective's hand and said, "You holding something in?"

"Knock it off," Caputo snapped. "Another couple of inches and I'd be crapping in stereo."

"Are you okay Tom?" Kane asked.

"Yeah," Caputo answered. "He grazed a cheek."

"With a target that big, he only nicked you!" another uniformed cop said.

"Come on Jack." Caputo took his friend's arm and started to walk him to the other side of the bridge. "Did I see what I think I saw?"

Kane nodded in the affirmative. "Yup. The son of a bitch jumped."

Caputo flipped his bloody handkerchief and kept walking. "I know that this is the lower level but it's still quite a drop to the river. And if you survive the fall, well you've got the logs and crap in the water and the current to worry about. Oh, and if you make it through all that, you'll probably get run over by a barge or riverboat."

They reached the other side and looked down. The Ghost's body was nowhere to be seen.

"I'd say that there's a good chance the asshole broke his neck," Caputo concluded. "Hitting the water from that height is like jumping into a parking lot from three floors up."

Kane winced at the thought. "Yeah… that would have to hurt."

"We'll send out the river patrol, but they probably won't have much luck. By the time they get up here it'll be dark, and if he is dead, his body will probably be a mile down river."

Suddenly a uniformed officer yelled to Caputo. "Hey Tom, it looks like your jumper friend had a finger shot off!"

"Yeah, we know!" Kane yelled back. "He lost it about seven years ago."

The cop looked confused and pointed to the ground. "Well then, I just found it and it's right here."

Kane and Caputo looked quickly to each other in disbelief.

"Another finger!" Kane seemed amazed.

Caputo grinned. "If he's alive, he's going to be pissed at you."

Kane looked back at the racing river.

"He's got to be dead."

Caputo was still smiling. "If he's not, he'll never play the piano again."

He paused for a second.

"You know this little flesh wound is starting to sting." He rubbed his fanny.

Kane looked back at Caputo.

"Let's hope it doesn't need stitches."

Caputo's eyes widened.

Epilogue

Jack Kane was tired. Not your ordinary tired, the way you feel when you stay up past your bedtime or work extra hours at the office. No, it was more the kind of tired that permeates to your core; that squeezes every ounce of energy and vitality from your very being. He needed to leave, to return to his home, his life and his bed. His personal batteries were drained and they desperately needed to be recharged.

This isn't to say that he didn't like Pittsburgh. Actually, he had grown very fond of the city. It's just that whenever the town's name was mentioned, he thought of hard work. For the time being, he had had enough of that. He wanted rest, relaxation and free time. Maybe he'd take a week or two in New England. He'd been thinking about spending some time in Newport or possibly Hyannis, on the Cape. No one would be shooting at him there. He'd be safer, the lobster would be fresh and the beer cold.

Caputo interrupted his friend's daydream. "Boy, you sure look beat, Jack. Didn't you get any sleep last night?"

Kane shook his head. "No, I was too wound up. I guess I really want to get out of this place."

The two men, who were sitting at the gate waiting for Jack's plane, were a sight to behold. Kane sat slouched and looked disheveled while Caputo appeared uncomfortable and seemed to favor the side of his derriere that hadn't been kissed by a bullet.

"I don't see why! I mean, you've only been running all over hell's bells chasing terrorists, defusing nuclear bombs and getting shot at! Sounds like a quiet weekend to me."

Kane just smiled.

"I'll bet you didn't see this much action, in such a short time, when you were with the NYPD!"

You're right," Kane agreed. "And I'm supposed to be retired."

"What fun would that be?"

They sat quietly for a couple of minutes and watched travelers pass by in front of them.

"You have to admit, Jack, that it's never dull around here."

"You're right about that. But I'll be honest with you, I'm kind of looking forward to some dull time."

"I don't blame you," Caputo said seriously. "Whoever would have thought that your coming out for an awards dinner would lead to everything that happened?"

"I know."

Caputo looked at his watch and to the gate. "They still haven't found his body."

"Is that normal?"

"He could be ten miles down river or snagged on the bottom, right where he jumped."

"What do you think? Will they ever find the body?"

"Probably. But only God knows when. Can you believe the asshole jumped?"

"Desperate times demand desperate measures."

"That was pretty desperate."

"What would you have done if it had been you?"

"I would have picked a bridge that was closer to the water."

Kane grinned and Caputo continued, "Seriously, I don't know if I could have jumped. You've really got to be crazy to step over that railing."

"Or confident you're going to live," Kane added.

"Yeah, but that's a long drop into a strange river."

"I think this guy is used to surviving situations like this," Kane went on. "I guess he just went too far."

"He went too far when…"Caputo stopped.

He was interrupted by, "Telephone call for Mr. Jack Kane. Mr. Jack Kane, please pick up the nearest blue phone."

"Oh great. They've probably canceled my plane," Kane said.

The tired man pulled himself out of his seat, and then found the nearest blue phone.

Caputo watched his exhausted friend pick up the receiver and place it to his ear. And as he observed his friend, he noticed a gradual change in Kane's body language. He didn't look tired anymore. From where Caputo was sitting, Kane seemed angry! Maybe they did cancel his plane, Caputo thought. Kane slammed the phone down, lowered his head, sighed heavily, and then slowly walked back to his seat.

Before Caputo could ask about the call Kane said, "Call off the search."

"What?" Caputo was confused.

"Tell the guys to stop searching the river. The bastard made it."

Caputo leaned forward in his seat. "That was him?"

"Yup." Kane answered. "He said that we'd meet again, sometime when I least expect it."

"Son of a bitch!" Caputo said emphatically. "What did you tell him?"

"I said, fine with me. I've still got eight more fingers to shoot off. He swore at me and hung up." Kane turned to his friend and smiled. "I don't think he liked that."

~ Finis ~

978-0-9841160-1-0

www.ingramcontent.com/pod-product-compliance
Lightning Source LLC
LaVergne TN
LVHW090944080826
845145LV00003B/888

* 9 7 8 0 9 8 4 1 1 6 0 1 0 *